The Girl Who Woke Up in the Morgue

By Stephen Rocco

This book is a work of fiction. Any resemblance to actual events or persons, living or dead, is entirely coincidental.

"The Girl Who Woke Up in the Morgue," by Stephen Rocco. ISBN 978-1-63868-073-4.

Published 2022 by Virtualbookworm.com Publishing Inc., P.O. Box 9949, College Station, TX 77842, US. ©2022, Stephen Rocco. All rights reserved. No part of this publication may be reproduced, stored in a retrieval system, or transmitted in any form or by any means, electronic, mechanical, recording or otherwise, without the prior written permission of Stephen Rocco.

*To my beloved late father,
Horace "Sonny" Rocco.*

Prequel

THE PEOPLE WHOSE JOB IT IS TO SAVE the lives of others navigated the tight staircase to the third floor, the clang of their bulky life-saving equipment drowning out their own labored breaths. One EMT said to his partner, "I hope it's not another overdose." This instinct seemed accurate as they hustled to save the young lady splayed on the couch.

To her rescuers who worked feverishly to revive her, they confronted a human juxtaposition. Her gray skin, the color of dark ice, felt clammy to their touch. Her long limbs were motionless but in a marathon pose, as if running away from the poison entering her body.

"It's no use," said the first EMT who had predicted the event as he watched his partner wordlessly continue his resuscitation attempts. Sweat poured from his brow onto the prone victim. Or were they tears? Gradually his movements slowed as the silent EMT offered his first words: "She's gone." Or was she?

Chapter 1:
The Awakening

SONNY FIORENTINO HEARD THE FAMILIAR SOUND of his cell phone going off at 3:00 a.m. As a funeral director, he knew it was common for folks to pass in the middle of the night. Sonny had a theory about the time of death. The overstressed body during daylight hours leads to an over relaxed body during the night. The tired heart simply stops in the quiet of the dark, especially for the elderly.

Sonny had a theory about a lot of things, which contributed to people viewing him as a bit peculiar. He often studied people's faces and asked them how they felt. These seemingly healthy folks would be astounded when Sonny suggested that they get a medical checkup. Frequently, these unsettled folks, given health information by a funeral director, would return to thank him for the detection of previously undiagnosed diabetes or a heart murmur. Folks often questioned how Sonny, at fifty years old, could live alone above his huge 19th century funeral home. Established by his great-grandparents in 1890, the business was located in a magnificent building, a historical pillared mansion with French stained glass windows that glowed at twilight, sitting atop the highest point in the town of Springdale.

Sonny's great-grandparents had done what he liked to do from his palatial nine-room apartment above the funeral home: look with pride at the "Springdocians" whom his family had served for generations. As it was now 2010, the family had served this community for 120 years.

At the other end of the cell phone call was a police officer, requesting Sonny's assistance. The officer, Skip LeBlanc, had been a classmate of Sonny's in high school. Skip sighed into the telephone that the deceased was a young woman who'd died of a drug overdose. Sonny replied incredulously, "Another overdose?" Sonny had buried several people in the last seven months under similar circumstances. Officer LeBlanc said that the EMTs had worked on the young woman for over an hour but could not detect a heartbeat. The coroner's

The Girl Who Woke Up in the Morgue

office decided not to examine her further, and she was ready for Sonny to pick up. "I am on my way, Skip," said Sonny.

After he prepared his stretcher, sheets and protective gear, Sonny climbed into his hearse. He then placed a call to his new funeral apprentice, Owen, to assist him. Sonny smiled as he recalled hiring Owen. Following the burial of his grandmother three months earlier, the young man had appeared at Sonny's funeral home. A recent graduate of Springdale High School, Owen said that something was triggered within him at the funeral. He was so impressed by Sonny and his staff's compassion, he thought he might like to go into the funeral business. An impressed Sonny hired him as a funeral apprentice but cautioned Owen that the business was not for everyone. This will be a good test for him, thought Sonny. He knew that not everyone could handle the death of someone, especially someone their own age.

Since it did not look like he would get married, Sonny had to consider that no children existed to take over the business when he was gone. Maybe it was hitting fifty, but lately Sonny had spent considerable time thinking about what would happen to the hundred and twenty year old business. "My nephew or niece might want it someday,"

Sonny thought, "but up to now they have not shown interest." This did not surprise Sonny, since most people averted this sad work. More than once, a bereaved family had said to him, "I don't know how you sit in this big house alone, Sonny, and do this work." He often agreed with them.

Arriving at an apartment building known to house many transient people, Sonny and Owen entered the decedent's living area. It was a small, one-room efficiency apartment with a combined tiny kitchen and living area. The decedent lay prone on the worn pullout couch. She lay on her face with one arm and one leg dangling off the couch, as if she was attempting to run and save herself. Her long, dark hair covered her face. Sonny gently pulled back her hair to examine her. The young woman had the angelic, unlined face of a twenty-something with a prominent nose ring on one nostril. Next to her outstretched hand was a glass of water and a bottle of pills.

Skip acknowledged to Sonny that he was saddened to keep meeting him under these circumstances. "We had two other deaths like this last week," sighed Skip, adding, "They are so young." Sonny nodded in silence, reflecting that he didn't realize the extent of these apparent drug-induced deaths. "I should have," thought Sonny, but he rationalized that he didn't bury all of the people. He made a mental note to call the three other funeral directors in town and check on their recent experience with these types of tragic deaths.

Skip told Sonny that young woman's name was Kelsey Jordan. The police were still tracking down any family members. As Sonny glanced down at the pill bottle, he noticed something. Skip seemed to read his mind as he commented, "I know. The label on the bottle shows that the pills were prescribed to a Julie Plummer. We are in the process of checking that out."

Sonny went about preparing who he now knew as Kelsey for the journey to his funeral home. He instructed Owen to clean the phlegm around her mouth and close an eye that was open. Next, they carefully wrapped her in a clean sheet and zippered her in a heavy canvas body bag. Then they delicately placed her on the stretcher and wheeled her into the hearse.

As Sonny prepared to drive to his funeral home, he looked down at the name of Kelsey's physician, Dr. Jerome Singer. Sonny had known this doctor's retired father, Dr. Stanley Singer, who'd had a thriving medical practice in Springdale. Sonny did not know his son Jerome, but was well aware of what he was doing in the community. In the short time since his father's retirement, Jerome had expanded their small family medical practice to include a comprehensive diagnostic and rehabilitation clinic. Sonny would have to talk to the younger Dr. Singer in the morning in order to obtain a signed death certificate.

Since Sonny had not been able to reach anyone from Kelsey's family, he told Owen that they would not embalm her that night. Sonny then instructed Owen to carefully unwrap the sheet, and they both gingerly placed the young lady on the large white ceramic embalming table. As they did, Sonny observed that Owen's face had changed. It was reddened and perspiring, and Owen gagged as if he were holding in a bad sneeze. "It's okay, Owen. You did a fine job. You can go home now. Make sure you wash up," Sonny spoke quietly to Owen. The new assistant said, "Thank you." As he headed to the washroom, he turned around, his face more relaxed. "I'm not sure this profession is for me, Mr. Fiorentino. I hope you understand." Sonny looked at the young man. "Of course, Owen. Don't be hard on yourself."

Sonny's interaction with Owen only reinforced his uneasiness entering the fiftieth year of his life. A poignant time, especially as his own dad had died at the age of fifty. "Maybe God has something bigger in store for

The Girl Who Woke Up in the Morgue

me one day besides burying the dead." Chastising himself for not seeing the benefits of serving the bereaved, Sonny's mind turned back to business. "I won't put her in the freezer tonight. Hopefully the family will contact me in the morning, and I can embalm her then."

Sonny glanced once more at the sight of the young woman who had no business being there. Her unlined face should have promised many more years of life. He shook his head sadly as he closed the lights in the morgue. He was just about to shut the door when he thought he heard a slight sound – almost like a sparrow ruffling its feathers. Probably nothing, he thought as he closed the door regardless, glad to go upstairs and finally get some rest after a busy night.

That sound remained in his ears, however. Almost halfway up the stairs of his home above the funeral chapels, Sonny turned around. He entered the morgue and walked over to Kelsey. He reexamined her, looking at her chest and nostrils, even putting a mirror over her nostrils. "I'm going crazy," thought Sonny as he chastised himself. Again he turned to leave the morgue. Just then a slight gurgle emanated from Kelsey. He ran over and saw her nose twitch, as if trying to remove something. She was alive!

Chapter 2: The Hospital

SONNY FUMBLED WITH HIS CELL PHONE as he nervously started CPR on the young girl. He dialed 911 in between breaks, and yelled into the phone, "Come to the Fiorentino Funeral Home morgue. I have a girl alive here." The dispatcher tried to clarify, "Is it someone attending a wake?" "No!" he shouted as he compressed her chest. "No, she is supposed to be dead. Hurry." This crazy dialogue continued for several exchanges until Sonny screamed, "Get the hell here as soon as possible!" hanging up the phone to concentrate on CPR. He focused on Kelsey. "Come on, Kelsey, stay with me," he said as he saw her chest compress and expand a bit stronger. She then made a gurgling sound

The Girl Who Woke Up in the Morgue

followed by a slight cough, as if she needed her lungs cleared.

Just then, the EMTs who had declared her dead an hour ago burst into the morgue. "I can't believe she's alive!" exclaimed one of them, his words expressing as much shock as nervousness. The EMTs then immediately used the defibrillator on her heart. Her breathing got stronger as they placed oxygen on her face and raced wordlessly to the hospital with Kelsey. Sonny was left alone in the morgue.

Overwhelmed by what had just happened, Sonny leaned against his preparation table, rubbing his head. He needed to feel something tangible to convince himself that what he had experienced was real. He guessed that he'd spent fifteen minutes performing CPR, but those minutes seemed like hours. Sweat coalesced on his neck, and he had the rubbery legs of an inebriated sailor. He went into the closest bathroom in his funeral home, the ladies' room, and applied lavender facecloths dipped in cold water on his face. He looked into the mirror, and dilated eyes as big as chestnuts stared back. He kept repeating, "I hope she is alright."

Unsure of what to do next, as it was now 4:00 a.m., Sonny made the journey from the basement of the funeral home where the morgue was located through the first floor, that contained three chapels, to his apartment on the third floor. He flopped on his bed fully clothed and tried to close his eyes. The scent of the young woman was still with him. Convinced he could never sleep tonight, he decided to go to the hospital.

When Sonny arrived at Mercy Hospital in Springdale, one would have thought it was midday. The chief of police and several officers were there, as well as several EMTs and an attorney for the ambulance company. A representative from the Medical Examiner's Office was also there. Sonny immediately thought they were there for reasons other than Kelsey's prognosis.

Sonny sidled over to Chief Frank Powell, Springdale's long-time police chief. "Any word on her prognosis, chief?" asked Sonny. "Nothing," said Chief Powell, "They are still working on her." Just then, one of the doctors came down the corridor. "Is anyone here from the girl's family?" asked Dr. Quigley. Chief Powell responded, "We have been unable to locate them. How is she doing?" Dr. Quigley said, "I think she is going to make it. We are trying to dilute the drugs in her body slowly, so I'm unsure if she has any permanent damage." Chief Powell gave a mournful chuckle and said, "I guess she wasn't ready to be buried." No one laughed.

Sonny asked Chief Powell if he had noticed a trend with the young people having a problem with prescription drugs. "Not really," he said. "We are mostly concerned about street drugs. We see a lot of cocaine and some heroin on the streets, but it's confined to a small group."

The chief then turned his attention to the circumstances which took place at the morgue. "Sonny, we should probably have you give a statement tomorrow at the station. We don't know where this is going legally." For the first time, Sonny considered that he may be at risk of liability, or at a minimum, bad publicity. Bad publicity was an alarming theme that his grandfather and father had drummed into him since his youth. He remembered their words: "In our business, you are taking care of a family's emotions as much as you are the body of their loved one. A family must have trust and confidence that their loved one is in good hands." Sonny realized that three generations of good will might be at risk here.

Sonny mentally retraced the events of the night since being notified of the death. He did think it was unusual that the medical examiner did not want to examine Kelsey before releasing her to the funeral home. In most cases, the medical examiner would do a post-mortem exam – at a minimum a toxicology report to see what drugs were in the deceased's systems. At most, a full autopsy to investigate any other suspicious symptoms in the body would have been performed.

Sonny knew that this was not his call to make. The medical examiner was responsible for Kelsey's body. Their office has tremendous authority to examine or not examine a decedent. Sonny laughed to himself, as he often compared the ME's powers to that of the IRS's decision to conduct an audit. In fact, he had some deaths where the family literally begged the medical examiner's office to do an autopsy, but they refused. For example, one family had alleged that the hospital caring for their elderly father was negligent and contributed to his death. After weighing all the circumstances, such as age, health, and the hospital report, the ME's office denied the family's request. Sonny had to tell this family that they could pursue a private autopsy at a teaching hospital, but that could cost from $5,000 to $10,000. Sonny had to consider that the ME's were getting so many of these drug deaths, they might be too relaxed in their inquiries.

The Girl Who Woke Up in the Morgue

Sonny's thoughts were interrupted by his friend, Officer Skip LeBlanc. "Amazing. I bet this is one for the books for you, Sonny."

"First time for everything, Skip, but I'm glad she's alive. She is such a beautiful girl."

Sonny asked Skip the same question he asked Chief Powell. Skip's response was different. "Yes," he answered, "I am seeing an upsurge in the amount of these drug cases. I hear kids say they can get twenty oxy for $20." Skip said he'd quickly learned that this stood for a twenty-milligram oxycodone for $20. "Some of these kids are getting these drugs from their grandparents' medicine cabinets.

Sonny told Skip that he had seen a sizeable increase in youthful deaths in the past year, but the death certificates did not list opiates. He noted that his two recent deaths were from heroin overdoses. Skip commented, "I'm not sure, but I think that kids are starting with opiates and graduating to stronger drugs."

For some reason, this conversation triggered something in Sonny's mind. He started to feel he was on the sad frontline of an epidemic that was destroying his community. He wondered if what was happening to

Springdale was happening in other communities, too.

As he returned alone to his silent funeral home, he was deep in thought about this issue. Climbing the three levels to his apartment, Sonny promised himself he would call his funeral colleagues in the morning. Maybe they had some answers for him.

Chapter 3: Sonny, the Funeral Director

Sonny woke up with a gnawing belly ache and the foggy head of one after a hangover. Carefully placing his legs on the floor, he looked at the clock: 6 a.m. He had slept only two hours. Hands rubbing his disheveled hair, Sonny had to convince himself that the young lady had really woken up in his morgue. Having just turned fifty, he said to himself, "I'm getting too old for this type of excitement." This recent pivotal birthday, even prior to the previous night's events, had left Sonny emotionally unsettled. He could not understand it. He had the largest funeral home business not just in Springdale, but in all the surrounding towns. His funeral home, purchased by his great-grandfather in 1890, was the nicest building in Springdale. This English Tudor mansion was purportedly built by a British loyalist in the 18th century. It sat atop the highest land in town, and the town's residents often looked up at sunset to admire the deep pitched roof, multiple gables, and chimneys that framed the horizon. Sonny had continually updated this historic building to resemble a serene museum, designed for the comfort of his bereaved families.

Sonny was groomed to take over the family profession. He was a fourth generation funeral director, all named Orazio, after his great-grandfather. Orazio I, Sonny's great-grandfather, was born in 1870, just after the Civil War. Like his own father, who had emigrated from the small village of Cirino, south of Naples, Italy, Orazio I was a carpenter. His father's carpentry business metamorphosed into building caskets to accommodate the multiple burials of Civil War veterans.

As a young boy, Orazio I, whose name was Americanized to that of Horace by his teacher, saw his dad interacting with these sad clients in his carpentry shop. Even as a young boy, the now-named Horace I thought these bereaved needed a more comfortable place to mourn. At the age of twenty, Horace I purchased the abandoned three-story mansion at the top of the hill, denying the neighborhood youths the fun of throwing rocks at the few remaining windows. His great-grandfather spent years restoring this property, and a Fiorentino had resided continuously in the building since 1890.

Sonny's grandfather, (Orazio/ Horace II), an only child, was born in 1900. He grew up in the restored mansion. The family resided on the third floor, in a large apartment that could accommodate a small wedding. It had four bedrooms, a library, and a dining room that could host a party of twelve. The second level was the main funeral home and included four dark wood mahogany chapels with adjacent sitting areas displaying antique paintings. The first level contained the livery, hearses, and limousines – as well as a medical morgue for preparation of the deceased.

Horace II had three children: Sonny's dad, Horace III, and two daughters. Like his father and grandfather, Horace III treated his work as far more than a business. Sonny had heard stories starting in grade school as to how the Fiorentino family had helped generations of Springdale residents. During the Depression, many grateful, bereaved families were allowed to pay a little each month for funerals until the debt was paid. Families suffering stillborn births or suicides were never presented a bill. Consequently, a reciprocal level of trust developed between the Fiorentino family and the community.

Sonny, or Horace IV, was born in 1960 and moved right into the funeral home from the hospital. He was joined by a younger sister, Lidia, born two years later. For some reason, Sonny's childhood friends quickly tired of pronouncing the name Horace. A grade school teacher called him Sonny one day, alluding to his easy disposition, and the name stuck. Today he did not even respond to the name Horace, given how infrequently he heard it.

Sonny grew to be a solid six feet, with dark curly hair, a large Roman nose, and a thick chin. That strong chin had a Fiorentino trademark – a deep dimple in the middle. Often called "a kiss from God", that dimple had been a staple of Fiorentino men for generations. At the age of fifty, Sonny's hair was now less curly, and more scalp appeared on his dome each year. Despite this, he had aged well, and many in the community could not understand how one of his female fans had not reined him in.

The Girl Who Woke Up in the Morgue

Sonny had a unique childhood that only a funeral family could understand. He and his sister often played downstairs, running between caskets on display in the showroom. His dad's mortuary workers often took him for ice cream in one of the company's limousines. Families with their loved ones in caskets downstairs came up after the wakes to have coffee and cookies made by his mother, Anna. Sonny often went to bed listening to bereaved family members talking and laughing with his parents in the dining room.

Sonny could recall the first time he saw his dad embalming a person. Wandering alone downstairs through the funeral home chapels, he heard noises from the morgue down below. Nervous, he normally avoided going down to the lowest level of the funeral home, as the morgue reminded him of a hospital. Calling out, "Dad," and hearing no response, he opened the accordion-like canvas door of the morgue. He peeked inside to see his dad applying something to a prone elderly woman who appeared to be sleeping on the white porcelain table. Clothed in a pink dress, the woman had styled hair and dainty earrings. His dad appeared to be putting lipstick on her, which he thought was strange.

"Dad," he called out again as the ten-year-old Sonny absorbed the scene. Startled, his father initially appeared irritated that his son was there. "I've told you not to come down here," he reprimanded. Mouth open, Sonny could not speak. He looked at the scissors, gauze, and tools carefully laid out, and his nostrils inhaled the sharp smell of medicine. He felt that a hospital existed in his home.

Then his father's demeanor softened as he seemed to study his son. "Do you know what I am doing here, Sonny?" he asked. Sonny shook his head. "I'm helping this family to remember their mother, how she was before she got sick." His dad had an obvious pride that his work provided a lasting image for the family. Sonny remembered that his father then stared closely at him, as if pondering whether his child could one day work with the dead. Sonny never forgot his dad's words: "It takes a special person to work with the dead, Sonny, and equally important, to work with the dead person's family, who are also in your care."

It was probably that passion that Sonny came to possess, which explained why the fifty-year-old Sonny never married. He started working wakes in high school, and eventually drove the hearse as soon as he got his license. Many nights in high school, he and his dad picked up decedents in the middle of the night, and Sonny was back in class the next morning. His dad was excited to talk about their future together in the business.

That was never to be, however. Following high school, Sonny attended an out-of-state mortuary school. One month before graduation, he got a tearful call from his sister. His father, only age fifty, had experienced a silent heart attack in the middle of the night and passed away. So silent was the death that it did not even wake his mother, Anna. Except for a recent diagnosis of type II diabetes, his dad had been healthy. His death was unexpected and traumatic. Sonny was a twenty-year-old, now in charge of the family business.

Unprepared to assume the myriad of details that running the funeral business entailed, Sonny spent his twenties learning everything he could. Many a night, his friends would be out doing what twenty-somethings do while he was working. Sonny later rationalized that he simply did not have time to both learn the business and pursue a relationship. It had probably contributed to him remaining single all these years.

The situation was further complicated when his sister Lidia got married right out of high school. She married her high school sweetheart, and soon had two children by the age of twenty-four. Like many youthful marriages, the character blemishes, which more mature couples examine, did not exist. Lidia's husband had limited job skills and developed a serious alcohol problem. By twenty-five, Lidia was divorced.

A dutiful Sonny assumed financial responsibility for his niece and nephew. Not wanting the family to live above a funeral home, Sonny helped them purchase a home in town. His mother moved in with his sister's family to help with the caregiving. By age thirty, Sonny was living alone in the massive cathedral-like funeral home on top of the hill.

As Sonny matured as a funeral director, he built up his funeral business. He never forgot the kindness of other funeral colleagues in the community when his father died. While an unskilled youth, Sonny relied on many of these older colleagues to show him how to obtain a burial permit, or to ship a decedent out of state. He never forgot that kindness, and did not view them as competitors, but rather as fellow death care professionals. Many times, he referred families to one of these colleagues when he was busy.

On rare nights, Sonny would lie in bed considering how things may have been different if his father had not died so young.

The Girl Who Woke Up in the Morgue

Sonny always wanted to get married and have children, but life had different plans. Even now, Sonny had not ruled out meeting a partner, but he had to admit that he had grown fussy in his older years. Maybe a woman would not like the way he kept house, or the food he ate.

When he let his mind wander during these mental ruminations, Sonny had to consider how grief may have affected his life choices. Why love someone when they can leave you so quickly, like his dad? Sonny was convinced his sister's decisions at eighteen were the result of their dad's sudden death. She simply wanted to move on from her pain, and her high school sweetheart relieved some of that pain. Even Sonny's mother had a perpetual sadness in her eyes, still there when she smiled. Anna absorbed her life into caring for her grandchildren but never cultivated many friends or hobbies. She often spoke of her husband in such idyllic terms that even Sonny teased her: "Yes, Ma, you married a saint." His mother did not laugh at this joke.

So at age fifty, Sonny had rationalized that his life was now pretty much set a certain way. Professionally superior, he had earned the respect of his community and the funeral profession. He operated the largest funeral home, not only in Springdale, but in the surrounding communities. He had a staff of ten, including three licensed funeral directors. He buried upwards of 400 deceased in an average year. He joked that his "families", those of the decedents whom he serviced, were enough family for him.

As Sonny sat at his kitchen table and aimlessly stirred his coffee, alone in his funeral castle, his mind returned to the young lady. He had many questions: How attractive were these damn pills? Why would such a beautiful girl risk her life so foolishly? Just who is this girl? As his mind ruminated on these subjects, Sonny again felt a heavy depression. "Maybe I should do something else with my life," thought Sonny. "No one knows how much time God has planned for them. I need to do something important for the living, other than burying their dead." Bursting with resolve, Sonny poured out his cold coffee. Enough of this sad stuff! I'm going to the hospital to see how the girl is doing.

Chapter 4:
The Girl in the Hospital

KELSEY FIRST HEARD A SOFT VOICE, accompanied by a strange hissing sound. She slowly opened her eyes to see bright lights and a handsome face emerge from this whiteness. The handsome face with dark features asked if her name was Kelsey. As she tried to speak, Dr. Gene Knight closed her mouth softly and told her to shake her head yes or no. He explained that she could not talk because she had a tube in her throat. Kelsey could now feel what seemed like a dry straw in her mouth. The doctor explained the tube was helping her to breathe. The good news was that her breathing was much better, and that her oxygen levels were nearly normal.

Dr. Knight smiled at Kelsey and said, "I think we can remove the ventilator now.

Would you like that?" She shook her head affirmatively. He then delicately removed the tube and intently watched her inhalations and exhalations. "You are a lucky lady", he said. "We are going to watch you for a few more days, but if all goes well, you can go home soon. Try not to talk for a bit. You know, you are quite a celebrity here." Kelsey was so tired, she did not know if she really heard him right. That "celebrity" remark faded in her mind as she dozed off.

She woke again to the familiar voice of her boyfriend, Taylor Jackson. Taylor and Kelsey had only been going out for a few months. He sat in her room with their friend Cheryl and his sister Sophia. She heard them laughing as a nurse told them to keep their voices down. Taylor looked at Kelsey and noticed that her eyes were opening. With a slight grin, he asked how she felt. Kelsey asked, "How did I get here?" Taylor laughed, "You don't know? You almost died in the funeral home." Kelsey looked puzzled. "I don't understand." "Everyone is talking about you!" commented an excited Cheryl. Then the friends went on to explain to Kelsey how she was found on the couch, and the EMTs declared her dead. And how she woke up in the morgue at the funeral home.

The Girl Who Woke Up in the Morgue

Kelsey was having trouble processing all this information. She slowly recalled Taylor crushing some pills and encouraging her to snort them. She remembered a feeling of nausea, and that was the last thing she could recall. Taylor laughed nervously and explained that she'd passed out on the couch with a smile on her face.

He said he then left to get some more pills, but when he came back, Kelsey was on the bathroom floor. "Your skin was bluish, and you had foam in your mouth. I didn't know what to do, so I put you on the couch and called 911."

Kelsey said weakly, "So you left me alone?" Taylor looked down at his feet. Sophia said, "No use both of you getting into trouble." Cheryl looked nervous as she said, "I need a smoke." The three looked at each other, and Taylor spoke first. "We'll be right back."

Kelsey's mind was spinning. Stunned, she thought, "I almost died from my stupidity." Just then she heard a slight knock at the door. A man with a genial, mature face entered her room. He smiled and asked, "Are you Kelsey?" She nodded. "I'm Sonny Fiorentino." Her quizzical reaction elicited from him, "I'm from the funeral home where you woke up."

Clearing her throat, Kelsey softly replied, "I guess you saved my life. Thank you." "No need for that," he laughed. "I think we both almost died." Sonny added, "How do you feel?" Kelsey croaked, "My throat is a little sore, and I feel like there's an elephant on my chest, but I'm glad I'm alive." "I am glad you are, too," said Sonny.

Just then both of them were distracted by the sound of a ruckus noise in the room. Taylor entered with the two women, arguing about where they would go for lunch. Taylor spotted Sonny, looked away, and mumbled, "Sorry." Kelsey introduced Taylor, Cheryl, and Sophia to Sonny, saying with a slight laugh, "He's my funeral director." Her friends did not get the joke and appeared uncomfortable. Sonny excused himself. "I'd better go, Kelsey. Okay if I check in with you every so often?" "Sure," she said with her easy smile.

Kelsey's friends perked up as soon as Sonny left. Taylor playfully rubbed her leg and said, "That's one of the people you want to sue. My friend said you should sue everyone who fucked this up – the EMTs, the doctors, and the funeral director." Kelsey hated when Taylor brought up schemes to make money. He was on disability for a back injury that happened over a year ago. She knew he could be sensitive with her alone, but when out with others, he always wanted to impress people. He told everyone he was starting college in the fall, but Kelsey knew that was untrue. She had quickly learned not to confront Taylor about these lies, as he had the ability to turn the emotional tables on her. She remembered when she'd once questioned him about the severity of his back injury, he'd accused her of being "ignorant," and she immediately felt guilty about raising the issue.

Kelsey did not feel like having a fight about whether she should file a lawsuit, so she feigned exhaustion. Her friends got the hint and loudly departed for their lunch.

All alone, Kelsey reflected on how badly her life had changed in the past year. It was no accident that she found herself alone in Springdale. She had grown up about a hundred miles away, in the town of Oxford. An only child, Kelsey was raised by her mom, Susan. She had little contact with her dad, Christopher Jordan.

Kelsey's mom, Susan Fulton, was the daughter of one of the most prominent families in Springdale. With roots in the town almost as long as that of the Fiorentinos, the Fulton Construction Company had built nearly the whole town. By the end of WWII, returning veterans relied on Fulton Construction to build their dream home under the GI bill. Block after block of homes built by Fulton dotted Springdale, and everyone could recite their slogan: "Fulfill your dreams with Fulton."

George Fulton, the patriarch of this family, founded the construction company in 1945. He had three children: George Junior, Harry, and Kelsey's mom, Susan. Following George Sr.'s death, George Junior and Harry took the company to even greater heights. Transitioning from home developments to commercial developments, the Fultons had numerous projects in Springdale and surrounding towns.

Since her earliest years, Kelsey had heard her mom disparage her family. On their infrequent car trips to Springdale, Kelsey would listen as Susan called her brothers "conceited assholes." Susan thought her mom, Grace, was the "queen" who was only concerned about the image of the Fulton name. The only person Kelsey's mom spoke well of was her late father, George.

As Kelsey got older, she pieced together the dynamics of the Fulton family. Her mother was the rebel of the family – always abusing curfews and choosing the wrong type of boyfriends. Her brothers, on the other hand, were the type of rule-abiding, serious youths who were destined to take over the family business.

As Susan grew into adolescence, her behavior worsened. She skipped school, had no relationship with her brothers, and began abusing drugs. She and her mother got into serious arguments that often turned physical. Her mother told her she was a "disgrace" to the family, and once yelled, "I regret having a third child." Her father was a peacemaker at home, telling his wife to have patience with Susan, as she was going through a "phase." George Sr.'s response to his daughter's "phase" was to buy her a new car when she turned sixteen.

Justified that she was an unwanted child, Susan's anger at the world increased. By senior year, she was suspended from school for threatening a teacher. Her parents, tired of endless parent/teacher and therapist meetings, essentially let her do whatever she wanted. After the school suspension, Susan was basically living with her motorcycle-riding boyfriend, Christopher Jordan. He lived alone with an alcoholic mom who rarely left her room. Unlike Susan, who had once been a stellar student, Christopher had had academic issues his whole life. His greatest enjoyment was tinkering with his motorcycle, and his secondary one was waking up to a joint.

Not surprising, at eighteen, Susan found herself pregnant with Kelsey. The dominant partner in the relationship, Susan demanded to know how Christopher was going to support the family. His dad, whom he had rarely seen, ran an automotive garage in the town of Oxford. He invited Christopher and his family to come to Oxford and offered to have Christopher train as an automotive mechanic.

So this was how Kelsey came to be born in 1992 and grow up as an only child in Oxford. Not surprisingly, things did not work out between Susan and Christopher. He was an indifferent worker who preferred long rides on his motorcycle and smoking joints on the road to fixing cars. His father eventually fired him, and the couple separated.

Susan's family reached out to her periodically in Oxford. But she told Kelsey that the family was "relieved" she was out of Springdale. Susan refused to accept their "charity" and also refused their offer of support. Eventually, Susan and Kelsey did secure public housing in Oxford. Susan supported herself on and off as a waitress.

As a child, Kelsey would visit the Fultons two or three times a year, particularly before Susan's father died. Susan would rant that she and Kelsey had to see the "assholes" to show

The Girl Who Woke Up in the Morgue

them that they were "respectable" family members. Kelsey recalled getting lots of presents from her grandparents and uncles.

Kelsey always had a distinct feeling she was different from her cousins. The adults seemed to work too hard to attend to her, almost with a sense of sympathy. She usually got more gifts than George or Harry's children. George had two daughters, and Harry had three sons, all younger than Kelsey. Among all the cousins, Kelsey got the impression she was the weird "black sheep" person of the family. Her cousins' finely tailored clothes and party dresses contrasted with Kelsey's blue jeans and only accentuated these feelings.

Chapter 5: Kelsey's Descent

KELSEY'S YOUTH WAS SPENT bending to the whims of her mother's personality. Susan was volatile and abrasive to her family and numerous boyfriends. Kelsey learned to adapt to her mother's moods. She became compliant, rarely demonstrating her own anger about a number of things that upset her. That included her mom's penchant for choosing "bad boy" types who had little in the way of job skills and even less insight into their own lives. Susan's relationships usually lasted three to six months; the longest lasted a year. These on-and-off relationships established a pattern for Kelsey. Her mom would be initially happy with a new boyfriend, invite him to move in, and then shortly after, berate him for some failure. Kelsey heard her mom yell out to at least five such boyfriends, calling each "a fucking loser" as he walked out the door. Kelsey did not bond with any of them.

Kelsey's happiest times with her mom were actually when she was in between boyfriends. Susan would spend more time with Kelsey, mother and daughter enjoying a girls' movie or playing checkers or Scrabble. But even during these good times, if Kelsey suggested seeing her grandparents or not needing another live-in boyfriend, Susan would explode. "I'm the only one who cares about you – forget my family."

Kelsey's personality in grade school and middle school mirrored her inner anguish. Always the "good girl," she rarely told others about her true feelings. Unable to afford braces, Kelsey had a slight overbite that made her self-conscious. She rarely smiled unconsciously and had a tendency to avert her gaze from the eyes of adults, including her teachers. Her mother's admonitions to "look people in the eye" made her even more self-conscious.

Susan's shifts as a waitress required her to work most evenings, which left Kelsey alone a lot. Graduating from various babysitters, she began staying alone by the age of ten. At school, Kelsey was a lackadaisical student who hated math. She did, however, love reading, and especially delved into happy novels about young girls with large families who lived in the country with goats and horses. She begged her mom for a pet, but the answer always was, "I can't afford another fucking mouth to feed." Kelsey daydreamed that one day, she would have the life of one of the young girls in the novels she loved.

In her solitude, Kelsey enjoyed sketching and painting portraits. Even Susan had to admit she had a talent for it. "That's the only thing you got from your loser father." She had to admit her mother was right about her dad. Kelsey remembered some visits with him when she was about four. She hadn't seen him since she started kindergarten, and had heard her mother rant that he'd moved to Colorado with his girlfriend. Her mom reminded Kelsey often that her "deadbeat" father did not pay child support.

In the solitude of her youth, Kelsey often drew faces of young, somber girls. They had big, blue eyes with long eyelashes, and in the rare times they smiled, the teeth were always perfect. They portrayed everything Kelsey did not see reflected when she spent hours staring at herself in the mirror. She often thought more people would love her if she was prettier.

The Girl Who Woke Up in the Morgue

Kelsey's life changed drastically at the age of fifteen. Her grandfather, George Fulton, passed away of a sudden heart attack. He was seventy years old. Kelsey's rare visits to Springdale ended. Her mom's outburst: "My fucking family even cut us out of his will." Susan and her daughter did not attend George's funeral.

Following her grandfather's death, Kelsey started receiving letters from her grandmother, Grace. At first, Susan would toss the letters in the trash. Kelsey retrieved them when her mother wasn't around, and she started a written correspondence with her grandmother. In the early letters, Grace simply asked general things about Kelsey: questions about school, boyfriends, etc. Eventually, Grace revealed that she regretted the chasm in the family. She even gave her version as to how the rift with Susan had occurred. Finally, Grace wrote that Kelsey's uncles and cousins missed her and wanted to be closer to her.

Kelsey made the mistake of asking her mother if she could visit the family in Springdale. Susan exploded, "They don't give a fuck about you. After everything I've done for you! Don't come home if you go there." Kelsey chose to accede to her mother's wishes.

Stephen Rocco

By Kelsey's senior year, two events transpired that affected Kelsey adversely. After being without a boyfriend for two years, Susan finally met Raymond Mignot, who quickly moved into the house. He was a huge drinker, and for the first time Kelsey witnessed her mother also abuse alcohol. Often Kelsey woke up to see both adults passed out on the couch, with empty Jack Daniels bottles and chasers surrounding the snoring adults. Dishes piled up in the sink, shopping grew scarce, and Susan lost her job due to frequent absences.

Often Kelsey went to bed listening to loud, incoherent talk and loud music disrupting her sleep. She smelled marijuana frequently, and even though she knew her mother used it to relax, Susan had never done it openly.

The other event occurred at Kelsey's graduation from high school. Her grandmother, Grace, asked if she could attend. Susan was adamant that Grace not attend. For once, Kelsey put her foot down and said, "Why not?" Susan's boyfriend Raymond chastised Kelsey for being selfish, and a huge row developed in the house. Kelsey slammed the door of her bedroom and waited for her mother to take her side for once. This never happened. Instead, another drunken party took place, with loud voices and the waft of marijuana filling the house.

Kelsey had started secretly talking to her grandmother around this time. Grace asked what she was planning to do after high school. Other than possibly attending some sort of art school, Kelsey had not put much thought into her future. Grace said that Springdale College had an excellent art school. She said that Kelsey could get a job in her uncles' property development business and take some art courses. They even owned some apartment buildings in the town and would let Kelsey live in one at no charge. Grace told Kelsey that all of the Fulton family looked forward to developing a relationship with her.

This offer appealed more and more attractive to Kelsey as her graduation approached. Raymond, Susan's current boyfriend, did not appear to be going anywhere, and the parties grew more and more boisterous. Susan seemed to be shifting her focus away from her daughter and toward her own happiness. Kelsey had never seen her mother hung over before, but now it was a common sight in the cluttered house.

Graduation night was a quiet affair. Susan seemed proud of her daughter: "You did something I never accomplished." Although Kelsey tried hard and had several casual girlfriends, she didn't receive any invitations to her classmates' home parties. Kelsey's mom didn't seem to notice the evening was marred by a quarrel that tipped Kelsey's ambivalent mind about leaving her mother's house. She recalled that her mom and Raymond insisted on wearing matching motorcycle jackets to the fanciest restaurant in Oxford. Despite Kelsey's arguments that the restaurant would not let them eat in that attire, her mother just laughed at her. "They will take our money, Kelsey, just watch." Instead Kelsey was aghast as her mother had a shouting match with the red-faced, French-speaking Maître D. Two of Kelsey's female classmates, celebrating graduation with their families, watched as Kelsey's mom erupted at the host. Kelsey was so embarrassed, and could feel them laughing at her without looking up. Kelsey's small group left the restaurant prior to the police's arrival. They ended up at the local McDonald's, where they celebrated Kelsey's graduation. Susan seemed to have no compassion as she told her daughter to "get over it," referring to the melee. Kelsey spent the evening listening to another drunken party hosted by her mother.

The next morning, Kelsey tiptoed through the living room adorned with beer cans. She placed a letter on the only open space she

The Girl Who Woke Up in the Morgue

could find on top of the television. On it, in red letters, she wrote, "Mom." Rather than having the inevitable confrontation with her mom, Kelsey had chosen the easier route. She explained that with the help of Susan's family, she was moving to Springdale. She hoped her mother could forgive her and would call her when her anger had subsided.

Chapter 6:
Kelsey arrives in Springdale

KELSEY HAD ARRIVED at her grandmother's Springdale home with little more than her suitcase. Her grandmother fussed over her and worked very hard to make Kelsey feel comfortable. She arranged visits with Kelsey's cousins: George's daughters, Grace and Alyssa, and Frank's sons, Owen, Max, and Parker. All were younger than she was, Grace being the oldest at sixteen, two years younger than Kelsey.

These visits were awkward for all, as Kelsey was essentially a strange adult that came into their lives. Kelsey got the distinct impression that everyone joined in these gatherings more to please Grandma Grace than anything else. Pointedly, neither her

The Girl Who Woke Up in the Morgue

grandmother nor her uncles asked about Susan.

Kelsey's uncles, George and Frank, looked resplendent in sporty "polo" chic attire adorned with flashy rings and gold jewelry. During Kelsey's interactions with them, they were bombarded with calls about one of their building projects. Invariably they would ask Kelsey a question, and be interrupted by another call. While they worked hard to be nice to Kelsey – almost too nice – their body language left Kelsey feeling like she was a nuisance to them.

During visits, her cousins talked to her briefly, and then invariably retracted to their grandmother's living room to play on their cell phones. Kelsey instinctually realized that her upbringing and theirs were quite different. Her cousins had the best clothing and the most up-to-date cell phones. They peppered their dads with requests to invite friends to their beach house. Kelsey picked up that her uncles also took their families on winter ski vacations.

Kelsey's oldest cousin Grace, named after her grandmother, was as self-absorbed as most privileged adolescents. Kelsey overheard her teasing with a girlfriend that one of their mutual "friends" had an old flip phone. Being a bit closer to Grace in age, Kelsey had hoped she might have more of a relationship with

Grace. One day she interrupted Grace at her favorite isolated spot at her grandma's desk. Normally Grace was texting or talking to one of her girlfriends, perched like a pretty doll, facing away from other family members. Kelsey asked if Grace would like to go to a movie or something with her one day on the weekend. Picking at her pink manicured fingernails, Grace mumbled something like, "I don't do movies." Kelsey surprised even herself and said, "Why don't we go to a museum? Have you been to the Kellogg Art Museum in town?" "Museum?" scoffed Grace. "I wouldn't be caught dead there." Kelsey was tempted to try a third option, but Grace had already dialed someone on her phone. As a defeated Kelsey walked away, she overheard Grace use the word museum and loser in her conversation, and then burst out laughing.

On another visit, for once, she sat alone with her uncles when they were not interrupted by business calls. George said that they did not think Kelsey should stay with her grandmother too long. They offered her a free studio apartment in one of their residential buildings and a job nearby in their business offices. "How do you like that, Kelsey? Does that sound good?" peppered George. Kelsey nodded her head, too intimidated to ask what her salary would be. Her uncle said, "My mom

The Girl Who Woke Up in the Morgue

said you might want to take some art courses at the local college." Kelsey nodded. "You might want to take some businesses courses too, right?" Again, she nodded. "So that settles it, then. Come in to work this Monday," instructed George.

When her family left, Kelsey was left alone with her grandmother, who was obviously happy about the plans made for Kelsey. No one had asked Kelsey about her thoughts. "I am going to buy you a car, Kelsey, a used one, to get around," Grace said. "I wanted you to stay here with me, but my sons disagreed . They want you to have your own space."

The night before her first day of work, Kelsey swallowed hard and called her mom. She had been gone for two weeks at this point. As expected, Susan was furious. "I can't fucking believe you would do this to me!" Kelsey tried to explain that she really was doing it to take art classes. Susan retorted, "Screw art classes. You did this to get something from my family." Susan hung up the phone.

After the phone call, Kelsey spent a restless night in her room. She felt like some sort of traitor to her mother. She also started to think that her relatives in Springdale felt "stuck" with her and were helping her out of pity. Kelsey never felt sadder or more alone in her young life. "What will happen to me?" she replayed over and over again in her mind until she fell asleep.

The next morning, Kelsey got up early to put on the business suit her grandmother had bought for her during their shopping forays. She straightened the dark curls which fell on her shoulders, thinking it would make her look more professional. After applying her makeup, she viewed herself, and then decided to remove the dark mascara on her eyes. "Not too much makeup is better," she thought. As she was leaving, her grandmother praised her appearance, adding, "Your grandfather would be proud of you." Kelsey was not sure of that, but she was pleased when she looked at her grownup image in the mirror.

Kelsey drove to the Fulton business office in her Grace-purchased used Camry. Kelsey's uncles were not there, but she was greeted by the long-time office manager, Ruth McGrath. A no-nonsense fifty something, Ruth explained Kelsey's job responsibilities, adding, "Even if you are a Fulton, you will be treated like everyone else."

Ms. McGrath assigned Kelsey to work with a similarly aged co-worker, Sophia Jackson. "Work hard, and don't ask too many questions," Ms. McGrath advised. The terrified Kelsey was relieved when finally alone with Sophia. "Don't worry," Sophia smiled. "Her bark is worse than her bite. She's been here so long, she thinks she owns the company."

For the first week, Kelsey worked closely with Sophia. She taught Kelsey some basic accounting principles – receivables, rents, etc. Kelsey learned that Sophia was to get a promotion now that Kelsey was hired to replace her. Kelsey's job would be to manage the maintenance of the extensive network of commercial and rental properties that the Fultons owned. If a heating problem arose, a tenant moved out, or a property needed painting, it would be Kelsey's job to assign staff to remedy these issues. With Sophia's help, Kelsey soon grasped the basic requirements of the job.

After the first week on the job, Kelsey moved into the small studio apartment provided by her uncles. She furnished her apartment with the help of her grandmother, who picked out most of the furniture. Kelsey's salary - $600 per week – afforded her to have her first savings account. To decorate her apartment, Kelsey framed and hung some of the portraits she had drawn. Her grandmother seemed genuinely impressed with Kelsey's work.

Unfortunately for Kelsey, time had slipped by, and since it was October of 2009, she was not able to enroll at the local community college to take art classes until the following semester. She would have to wait until January to pursue her dreams.

So Kelsey immersed herself in learning the nuances of her job. Even Ms. McGrath gave a tepid compliment to Kelsey that she had not "messed up once." Kelsey was appreciative to the Fulton family for helping, but she felt increasingly alone in her apartment.

On occasion, Kelsey saw her uncles at the business office, but that was the extent of their contact. Some Sundays she would have dinner with her grandmother, but her cousins were rarely there. Ski season had just started, and the Fultons went to their winter chalet on weekends. Kelsey was not invited.

In retrospect, the downfall of Kelsey's living in Springdale as an eighteen-year-old was that she did not know anyone. She occasionally went to art shows alone on weekends, but she spent considerable time watching television. She constantly worried about how her life would turn out. She asked herself a lot of questions: "Would she fall in love?" "Was she worthy of love?" "Would she have children?" "Would she be a better mom that her mom had been?"

The Girl Who Woke Up in the Morgue

Sophia, her co-worker, was really her only social contact. Sophia was a year older than Kelsey and had an easy-going demeanor. Diminutive, with dark curly hair, Sophia could pass for Kelsey's sister. As Halloween approached, Sophia invited Kelsey to a party at her home. Having graduated from Springdale High School the year before, Sophia had invited many of her high school friends. Kelsey was excited but asked Sophia if people would be drinking alcohol at the party. Kelsey explained that she did not want to be part of a drinking scene. "Of course not," Sophia remarked.

The night of the party, Kelsey dressed up in a special costume she had designed herself. She would be dressed as Cat Woman in a slinky costume that accentuated her trim figure. She teased her hair, and wore whiskers, all of which gave her a dark feline look. Kelsey was excited as she drove to Sophia's home, excited to finally be with friends her own age.

Kelsey entered Sophia's apartment, which she shared with her older brother. She was surprised at the mature faces she saw at the party. While some appeared to be Kelsey's age, many of the people there looked to be in their mid to late twenties. Everyone had alcohol. There seemed to be two different parties—one upstairs, where Kelsey entered, and one downstairs in the basement where people continually descended. Loud music pervaded the home, and Kelsey grew nervous. This party felt and sounded like the ones at her mother's home.

Sophia welcomed Kelsey, winking slyly. "I told you there would not be *too much* alcohol." She introduced Kelsey to some of her high school friends before excusing herself and going downstairs. Kelsey stood self-consciously with Sophia's classmates, who talked about life after graduation.

"Hey, Cat Woman." Kelsey heard these words and turned to see the handsome face of a stranger. Tall, with black curly hair like Kelsey, the man said, "I like your costume." Since he did not have a costume, Kelsey asked, "What happened to yours?" He responded with a grin, "I am in costume. I'm a drug dealer." He said it so casually, Kelsey considered the comment a poor joke. Seeing Kelsey's expression, he quickly added, "You must be Kelsey. Sophia told me about you – she's my sister. I'm Taylor." To Kelsey's surprise, she and Taylor embarked on an easy conversation. He also liked to draw – landscapes rather than portraits – and seemed interested in her desire to take art classes. "Maybe I can join you there." Over the next three hours, Kelsey eased into a comfortable dialogue with Taylor. Kelsey even shared her difficult youth with him, as well as how she happened to be living in Springdale. They danced together, and before Kelsey knew it, it was 1 a.m. Taylor walked her to her car and asked if he could see her again.

Over the next month, Kelsey spent considerable time with Taylor. He had a sensitive side, despite his rather tough appearance. He was tall and lean with a partial beard that stubbornly would not grow in fully. Kelsey thought him to be "rock star" handsome but was a bit intimidated by his appearance. He had numerous tattoos on his arms, one color merging into another, depicting images Kelsey could not decipher. His long, curly hair normally hid the multiple earrings he wore on his ears. His ten fingers were adorned with various types of metal rings. His normal attire was jeans, black boots, and a leather vest. Despite this tough visage, Taylor was so easy to talk to that Kelsey shared with him some of her deepest insecurities.

In time Kelsey learned that Taylor and his only sibling, Sophia, had an upbringing similar to her own. Now twenty-one, he had dropped out of high school largely because he'd attended ten different schools in his youth. His family had moved so often that he and his sister never felt settled in one place.

Stephen Rocco

His largely absent father, both emotionally and financially, left him and his sister dependent on their mother. Although she tried, their mother became an alcoholic who formed relationships with similarly damaged boyfriends. Sophia and Taylor would periodically move into their maternal grandparents' Springdale home in between their mother's separations from men. But invariably, they would return to living with her. In his sophomore year, Taylor and his sister permanently went to live with their grandparents. This move was because the courts intervened when their mother was charged with neglect following her numerous failed efforts at treatments. Their grandparents became Taylor and Sophia's guardians, and they lived there until Sophia graduated from high school, when brother and sister moved into their own apartment. Finally able to be on their own, Taylor and Sophia had guilty feelings about disrupting their grandparents' "golden years."

Kelsey enjoyed spending time with Taylor, and by December her identification and comfort with him led to her first true relationship with a boy. Sophia was thrilled with her brother and friend's budding friendship. Every week there would be a party where all three were invited. Although Kelsey

The Girl Who Woke Up in the Morgue

and Taylor would occasionally go to a movie, weekends were for one, possibly two, parties. Kelsey even started to drink a glass of wine at these parties. But Taylor and his sister were far beyond a glass of wine. They loved to dance and drink extensively. On occasion, brother and sister were so intoxicated that Kelsey had to drive them home and help them into their apartment. However, Kelsey still looked forward to time spent with her friends, as much to combat her sense of isolation as anything else.

Christmas holidays were spent at Kelsey's grandmother's home, the Fulton affluence on full display. Expensive gifts were shared with one another. While Kelsey received a number of expensive gift certificates from her grandmother and uncles, she could not shake the feeling that she was still an outsider.

Kelsey looked forward to attending a New Year's Eve party with Taylor at the home of his boss. This event had special significance to Kelsey, as just before Christmas, she had been intimate with Taylor. This was Kelsey's first sexual experience, and it reflected her growing trust in Taylor. She was amazed that someone could love her despite how lonely she felt inside. Taylor, with his sensitivity and understanding, was unleashing feelings in

Kelsey that she'd never experienced before. Aware that Kelsey was a virgin, Taylor was especially patient with her during this first encounter.

The night of the New Year's party, Kelsey excitedly prepared to spend a second night with Taylor. The spacious townhouse apartment was festive – liquor bar in one corner, food in another. There were balloons and loud music in each room. Taylor said that this luxury apartment was owned by his boss, "Doctor C."

The party was unlike anything Kelsey had seen in her young life. She estimated that over one hundred people were in attendance. Many of them looked to be in their thirties. Taylor introduced one of these individuals to Kelsey as "Doctor C", the host of the party. Over six feet tall, Doctor C had a completely bald head that looked like it had been polished. He had deep, dark eyes, and a mouth framed by an equally dark moustache and goatee. He reminded Kelsey of her uncles – well-dressed, impressed with themselves, and not interested in anything said by someone else. She watched as Taylor deferred to this man in a behavior she had not seen in him before. She observed an unusual vibe between these two that disturbed her.

The Girl Who Woke Up in the Morgue

As the party progressed, Kelsey, excited about her desire to be alone with Taylor, drank more wine than normal. Not seeing Taylor, she wandered to the downstairs pool room. There she saw Taylor and Doctor C huddled with a group of friends. Feeling a bit giddy with wine, Kelsey interrupted the conversation and asked with a smile, "How do you afford this apartment?" The host replied tersely, "That's my business!" Embarrassed, Kelsey ran upstairs. Taylor chased after her and wrapped his arms around her. "What was that all about?" questioned a tearful Kelsey. Taylor consoled her. "He's a strange guy, don't worry about him." Taylor walked Kelsey out on the patio to get fresh air. Kelsey persisted, "Who is that guy?" "Look, Doctor C, gets stressed out sometimes. He runs a big business. But let's forget about him." He gathered her in his arms and gave tearful Kelsey a passionate kiss.

Taylor reached into his pocket and pulled out two pills. "Here, take one. It will make you feel better." "What is it?" asked Kelsey. Taylor put the pill in her hand. "It's a prescription pill that will make you feel better. Here, I'll take one with you." Kelsey reluctantly placed the pill in her mouth and continued talking with Taylor. Almost immediately she got lightheaded, and a strong feeling of contentment saturated her body. Forgotten was any worry about the "Doctor C" incident. Rather, Kelsey experienced an inner euphoria that removed all her worries and insecurities. She felt a confidence that replaced the insecure Kelsey. She felt that she was the master of her environment. Kelsey could not understand how this one pill made her feel so confident. She later replayed over and over in her mind what was so attractive about this first pill. The best she could define her experience was that she felt like a soaring hawk — king of the skies, far removed from the shitty world below her.

Kelsey spent a wonderful night with Taylor that was the pinnacle of her life. When they awoke, Kelsey asked Taylor what was in the pills they took. He explained that the pills were perfectly legal oxycodone. They had been prescribed by a doctor. Kelsey asked if he had more pills. She wanted to experience whatever this pill did to her again. Kelsey spent New Year's Day of 2010 in Taylor's arms while consuming two more "oxy" pills.

As the new year evolved, Kelsey could not wait to get out of work to share a pill with Taylor. She soon learned that Sophia also took these pills, along with her high school friend Cheryl. Weekends were spent taking other pills - some of which gave Kelsey a different experience than oxycodone. When the oxys gave her too intense a high, Taylor gave her

The Girl Who Woke Up in the Morgue

Xanax pills to calm her down. Sometimes, after a long weekend of partying, Kelsey needed something to help her get to work on Monday. Taylor gave her pills such as Adderall or Dexedrine, which jump-started Kelsey in the morning. Kelsey began to notice that the pills came from prescription bottles with names of people she did not know. But at this point, she didn't care whose pills she was taking – she just needed that rush.

Along with knowledge about these pills, Kelsey soon learned how Taylor afforded his apartment. Taylor had not lied at that Halloween party – he sold pills for a living.

By the end of February, when Kelsey was supposed to be enrolled in art classes, she was only interested in capturing the euphoric feeling of those first pills. Kelsey quickly found that it took more pills, and of higher strength, to recapture the feelings of New Year's night. She learned that the 30 mg oxys worked three times quicker than the 10 mgs. She also needed other drugs to take her up, or down, depending on the situation.

It wasn't long before these pills took over Kelsey's life. By April, Kelsey was frequently dizzy and had trouble concentrating at work. Ms. McGrath found her asleep at her desk one day and reprimanded her. After that, Kelsey had a ready supply of "uppers", supplied by

Taylor, to get her through the day. If she got anxious at night, she took Xanax or valium to relax her. Weekends were spent at her apartment or Taylor's taking oxys, Percocets, or Vicodin.

Kelsey soon found it harder and harder to secure the deep high she had once experienced with these pills. She'd watched Taylor crush the pills to receive a deeper high, but up until this point, she had resisted this approach. On the night Kelsey woke up in the morgue, she had felt awful all day. She had vomited and had trouble walking. The pills Taylor gave her did not seem to do anything for her. When Taylor arrived at her apartment, he suggested crushing the pills, as much as to relieve these symptoms as for a high. The last thing Kelsey remembered before waking up in the hospital was inhaling the crushed pills in Taylor hands.

Chapter 7:
Dr. Singer's Denial

SONNY FIORENTINO WALKED INTO the plush office of the Springdale Pain and Family Clinic. An impressed Sonny had to admit that his old friend's son, Dr. Jerome Singer, had brought the practice to great heights. His dad, Dr. Stanley Singer, had retired a couple of years earlier. Sonny had a lot of respect for the elder Singer, who was good friends with his own dad. One day as a boy, Sonny had accompanied his dad to Dr. Stanley Singer's office to get a death certificate signed. He recalled telling his dad on the ride home that the doctor's office wasn't nice. His dad cautioned with stern eyes, "Don't judge a book by its cover, son. That man has helped many people in his time, often taking no payment for his services." Sonny had never forgotten that conversation, and when he got older and secured his own death certificates from the distinguished doctor, Sonny realized how right his father was.

"I'm here to get a death certificate for the Fulton boy," Sonny said to the harried receptionist. Sonny soon realized why she appeared so harried. Patients were going in and out of the offices, while administrative staff behind the receptionist were discussing insurance reimbursements. The death certificate was quickly located. Sonny asked, "Do you think I can talk to Dr. Singer for a moment? I'm Sonny Fiorentino, a funeral director in town." The frown on the receptionist's face told him that it was one more task for the overworked woman. "Please take a seat. As you can see, we are very busy today," she said tersely. "Thank you," said Sonny, seating himself comfortably in a plush chair.

Sonny looked admiringly at his lavish surroundings. He felt he was in a modern hotel lobby rather than a doctor's office. He estimated that there were twenty fashionable patient chairs surrounded by pleasant hues of ocean-blue walls and rich gray rugs. He laughed to himself, recalling his conversation with his dad. "I can't complain about this office."

The Girl Who Woke Up in the Morgue

Sonny was surrounded by fifteen or so antsy patients sitting on the edge of their chairs, hoping their names would be called. He could not help noticing that many of these visitors were young – some in their 30s and 40s. Sonny's thoughts were interrupted by the pleasant face of Dr. Jerome Singer. "Sonny, it's been a long time. I haven't seen you since I worked at your funeral home."

Sonny instantly recalled that the summer before Jerome went off to college, he had worked as a landscaper. He recalled that Jerome was smitten with some of the things he saw at the funeral home. Jerome had asked about the type of walnut that adorned his chapels, or whether the gables were lined with bronze or copper.

Sonny had to admit that this Dr. Singer was no longer the scrawny kid going off to college. He had the distinguished features of his dad, but the resemblance stopped there. While his dad wore rumpled suits that were sizes too large, this Dr. Singer wore a finely threaded suit stretched tightly over his athletic physique. Gucci eyeglasses above a neatly trimmed Van Dyke presented an impressive appearance, accentuated by his easy smile. "How have you been, Sonny? You look great; still living alone in that beautiful funeral home?" Sonny smiled. "Haven't found the right one yet, doctor. Any chance I can talk to you alone? It will only take a minute." The ever-present smile briefly left Dr. Singer's face, and he quickly glanced at his gold Rolex. "Okay, sure, come with me. Anne, please hold my calls for a bit. Thank you."

Sonny was ushered into Dr. Singer's spacious office decorated with nautical pictures. One photo showed Dr. Singer with two children, a boy and a girl, whom Sonny estimated to be eight and ten. They were standing in front of a boat... Sonny corrected himself. This was not a boat, but a yacht. Dr. Singer sensed Sonny's admiration of his yacht. "She's a beauty I know, but I need a bigger one. I've outgrown her." Sonny got the sense that it mattered to Dr. Singer that people admire his success.

"Well, Doc, the reason I am here is because I have been burying a lot of young people lately. I buried four young people in the last six months alone. All of them died of drug overdoses. Many seemed to get hooked on medication that they found in their parents' medicine cabinets. I was curious if you have seen the same thing?" Dr. Singer took off his eyeglasses and rubbed his eyes as if pondering the question deeply. "I don't see it in my practice, Sonny. I will say there is considerable research into this new class of drugs called

The Girl Who Woke Up in the Morgue

opiates. They are not addictive. The problem, Sonny, is when people abuse the drugs and take too many. Obviously, doctors can't control that."

"It's funny you said the word control," answered Sonny. "The families burying these young people said their loved ones lost control very quickly. I mean, their children became addicted almost overnight. Some appear to have graduated to stronger drugs like heroin quite quickly."

"I don't see it here, Sonny. All I know is those patients you see outside are getting better relief than the ones my father treated, who lived in pain." With that, Dr. Singer stood up and said, "Keep me informed, Sonny, if it continues to be a concern." Sonny sensed the conversation was over and got up to leave. "I will, doctor. Thank you for your time."

Dr. Singer took a moment before calling Anne to bring in the next patient. He allowed himself a rare moment of satisfaction as to how far he had expanded his father's practice. Despite Sonny's concerns, he did not feel one bit guilty for treating many of his patients with these drugs. When opiates appeared in the medical journals in the late 1990s, they had been thoroughly tested. Even federal regulators concluded these opiates were not addictive. To Dr. Singer, it was the abuse of this wonderful pain medicine that was the problem. Dr. Singer rationalized that the abusers were damaged souls who often had a litany of physical and emotional problems.

Dr. Singer's fascination with the profit involved in pain medication started in the early 2000s. Each day, opiate manufacturer representatives inundated his office with solicitations. Soon these companies hosted Dr. Singer and his wife on all expense-paid trips to some exotic Caribbean island. Not only did the companies wine and dine Dr. Singer, but they also offered him a "speaker fee" of up to $10,000 while on one of the trips. These "speeches" would often take place around Ritz Carlton pools, where Dr. Singer touted a particular brand of opiate to his physician colleagues.

Dr. Singer saw that in this desperate opiate competition, companies would pay higher and higher fees to doctors who used their particular product. The more they ordered, the higher their fee. In addition, companies rewarded Dr. Singer with higher bonuses for ordering higher strength pills. For example, his stipend was three times more when he prescribed a 40 mg OxyContin as opposed to a 10 mg tablet.

The Girl Who Woke Up in the Morgue

Soon, Dr. Singer was ordering opiates for nearly every complaint raised by his patients, from headaches to weak shoulders to creaky backs. By 2003, Dr. Singer's income from pharmacies alone was over $400,000. He saw no downside to an emphasis on helping patients alleviate their pain.

By the time the doctor's father retired in 2003, the younger Dr. Singer was sold on a new business model. Since he was a young boy, he had wanted to be a physician—but not a doctor who made house calls in a beat-up car. No, he'd worked hard to fulfill his dream, and now he was going to reap the rewards of his hard work. Once, when he was a young boy accompanying his father to a patient's home, he asked his dad why they didn't have a house on the lake like many of his friends had. His dad simply said, "One house is enough, son." Jerome watched his tired dad return into the home with his shirt invariably hanging out of his belt, and just shook his head.

As Dr. Jerome Singer relied more and more on the pain aspect of his practice, he quickly harnessed the various sources of his new profits. Patients with bad backs required full blood workups and x-rays. Insurance companies and federal agencies such as SSDI routinely paid for the tests, as well as the pain prescriptions. Soon Dr. Singer began charging patients for continued workups even when he did not perform them on patients.

By 2005, Dr. Singer's income was well over one million annually. His whole aura symbolized wealth. He added a pinky diamond ring to the hand that held his Rolex. A black Bentley sat in the driveway of his new 6,000 square foot home. And, yes, he purchased a house on the lake.

If Dr. Singer had any foreboding about his new business model, he realized his success was being mirrored by ambitious physicians all over the country. He read in medical journals that by 2005, the number of OxyContin prescriptions in the United States rose to more than 14 million – up from 316,000 prescriptions in 1996. This figure represented three billion in sales to pharmaceutical companies, compared to 44 million in 1996. Dr. Singer rationalized, "There is no reason why I can't capitalize on these medications."

By 2006, Dr. Singer's office could not accommodate his growing clientele. Word had spread quickly in the Springdale community that Dr. Singer could handle a variety of ailments with medication. He called in his friends, the Fultons, to design a state-of-the-art medical building, which he named the Springdale Family and Pain Clinic. Within a year he had hired three other physicians and several administrative staff. The office was constantly buzzing with a revolving door of new and old patients, and the processing of insurance claims from both private insurers and the federal government. In 2006 alone, his office processed over a million dollars from insurance claims – largely for medical exams and workups related to pain treatment.

Around this period, Dr. Singer sensed some ambivalence from his three physicians about the emphasis on pain medication. This same ambivalence he had revolved in his own mind some time ago. In Dr. Singer's mind, he was providing sound medical care and saw no downside to his operation. He even rationalized that he could renew prescriptions for his existing patients without seeing them. Naturally, he billed insurance for an office visit, and he encouraged his staff to do the same.

One day he overheard one of his doctors complain that their clinic was nothing more than a "pill mill." Dr. Singer convened a meeting of his physicians at once. "Look, you are doing well here financially – better than you would working at Springdale Hospital. If you have a problem with the direction of my practice, you are free to leave. I have no problem with our patients' care. Their medications are not addictive, and the only ones having problems are ones abusing the drugs. Many have never felt better. Besides, if we don't focus on these medications, some other practices will. The future is unlimited, and there is no downside."

Whatever ambivalence his three physicians had up to that point evaporated. Whether it was Dr. Singer's passion, or simple greed, the doctors were on board. If anything, they became more generous with prescriptions, even when clients came in with specific requests for Vicodin or Zanex. Soon the doctors agreed to open a pain clinic in the nearby town of Greenville. Unlike the lavish Springdale office, the Greenville clinic was located in a strip mall. It had two doctors and was conveniently located next to Greenville's only pharmacy.

What Dr. Singer's medical partners had not known was why his motivation to prescribe more pills had taken on greater urgency. A too-close relationship with his twenty-something medical secretary had led to a full-blown affair. The torrid six-month affair made Dr. Singer feel young again, but came at a painful price. His wife of fifteen years discovered his infidelity. His perfume-laden Armani suits led to a separation and an acrimonious divorce. His 2008 divorce came

The Girl Who Woke Up in the Morgue

with a $15,000 monthly child support order, among other perks, such as tennis club membership and private school tuition for his children. Combined with his own living costs, plus the price of impressing the many women he dated, Dr. Singer's expenses surged.

Making well over a million dollars a year, Dr. Singer amazingly realized that he needed still more. One day, in a lull in the whirlwind of patients he saw each day, Dr. Singer came upon a solution. "I need more patients." He computed that his offices currently issued over 1,000 prescriptions per week. He could easily double those prescriptions.

Whatever concerns he once had about any harm coming to the community from these pills had been resolved years earlier in Dr. Singer's mind. Besides, he had his eyes on a new 60 foot Sun-Seeker to replace his current yacht. Sonny Fiorentino's worries were the last thing on the doctor's mind.

Chapter 8: Business Partners: Dr. Jerome Singer and Bobby C AKA Dr. "C"

IT WAS PROBABILITY THAT two outsized egos like Dr. Jerome Singer and "Doctor C" would cross paths in Springdale. Each loved the good life, needed money to support that life, and had the intelligence to achieve it.

Dr. Singer later recalled that they first met in early 2008. An eligible bachelor now, Dr. Singer often found himself in the Radius Nightclub late at night. He would have had to be blind not to notice the imposing Doctor C — who was ever-present, his bald head a contrast to the dark lights of the intimate club. From supervising staff to attending to the needs of the band, Doctor C's alert eyes did not miss

The Girl Who Woke Up in the Morgue

much. Years in the nightclub business had trained him to see trouble, but more importantly, potential trouble. Often that included catering to law enforcement personnel, who always got a free drink from Doctor C.

Years managing music acts had also put Doctor C in the drug business. Not Doctor C himself, whose strongest drug was good whiskey. But managing bands in the "go-go" 80s and 90s included getting cocaine for band members. Doctor C was careful to reward the band with their drug of choice after their performance. By 5 a.m., these same musicians needed help to get some sleep before their next performance. As a result, Doctor C became knowledgeable about a new class of sedatives called Benzodiazepines. He routinely handed out tablets of these sedatives, more commonly called valium, Xanax, and Klonopin.

In the late 1990s, his bands started asking Doctor C for different drugs. A confused Doctor C saw these drugs coming out of pockets or purses in prescription bottles. The ever-curious Doctor C did some investigation into these pills commonly known as opiates.

He learned around this time that scientists had been able to combine natural opium with synthetic agents to form a new type of semisynthetic drug. Society labeled this class of drugs Oxys, but their legal name might be oxycodone, oxymorphone, hydromorphone or hydrocodone.

Whatever they were called, Doctor C realized quite quickly that the drugs worked. Whatever the attraction was, users wanted more and stronger amounts of these drugs. The ambitious Doctor C soon calculated that behind this simple pill lay piles of money.

Initially, the street value of these pills was $10 per mg. Doctor C quickly learned the drug vernacular lingo: 10 mg of "whites" sold for $10; 20 mg, known as "bananas," sold for $20 per pill, and the higher dose 30 mg "blues" sold for $30 or more. Eventually, the pills were made as high as 90 mg and higher, which netted even more revenue.

The astute Doctor C did some math calculations. He learned that some old-time doctors in Springdale could be convinced to write prescriptions for up to 300 pills at one time. If he sold these oxys for $20 per pill, he had a profit of nearly $6,000. His mind went to the ease of getting fistfuls of these scripts and the new unlimited earnings. And for Doctor C, the best part was that these drugs were legal. Unlike cocaine, which came with severe legal risk, the risk in selling these legal drugs was minimal.

The Girl Who Woke Up in the Morgue

By 2008, Doctor C had built a virtual pill empire in Springdale. Employing a small group of people he called marketers or recruiters, they aggressively sought out people to buy scripts. His recruiters paid anyone from college students to retirees $300 for getting a legal prescription. They also preyed on the elderly or disabled to sell them their own pills. Doctor C's staff directed these people to friendly doctors and pharmacists in Springdale. These people, known as "runners," would then get the pills in the hands of street dealers or brokers who sold the pills to customers.

A favorite technique of Doctor C was to get disabled people on SSDI or government assistance to get scripts. With these patients, the shrewd Doctor C did not even have to pay for the prescriptions. The government would reimburse the pharmacy for the medications. Doctor C could not believe the ease of his business. By 2008, after expenses to his staff, he raked in $400,000 per year. Doctor C enjoyed nothing more than returning to his family's New Jersey home driving his new Bentley.

Doctor C was making so much cash that he needed a separate business to launder the money. A colleague at the nightclub who owned a small garbage pickup business soon found that he had a new partner in Bobby C.

The business "Springdale Waste Management" was the perfect vehicle for laundering the vast amounts of cash that Bobby C received. Filtering the money through the business "cleaned" the cash, allowing him to legitimize the income.

It was during this pivotal period of 2007 that Doctor C and Dr. Singer crossed more intimate paths. By coincidence, the men found that their boats were moored next to one another at their yacht club. Doctor C was impressed by both the size of the doctor's boat (it literally dwarfed his own) and the parade of young ladies who arrived on weekends. Soon Doctor C was a regular member of the weekend parties that left both men with hangovers.

It was during one of these boat-rocking Sunday morning chats that their conversation turned to business. Sipping coffees to ease the alcohol-induced headaches from the previous night's party, the friends first talked about drugs: specifically, the burgeoning opiate business.

Like two cold-eyed sharks circling prey, the men learned that they were in the same business. And by a serendipitous stroke of luck, their needs to expand their businesses fit perfectly. In Doctor C's eyes, he no longer had to find friendly doctors or pharmacists to

The Girl Who Woke Up in the Morgue

obtain the pills. Two elderly physicians that Doctor C routinely used in his business had died. He had hoodwinked these clueless doctors into selling their prescription books with their signatures pre-signed.

Dr. Singer was fascinated by the sophistication of Doctor C's street distribution hierarchy. The doctor marveled that recruiters roamed the streets, constantly churning up new clients – many of whom were on government or disability insurance. Dr. Singer saw the natural connection of the runners – the people who took the patients to the doctors and pharmacy- to the brokers, who then distributed the pills on the street. Dr. Singer did some mental calculations with his new friend. "I currently push out about 1,000 prescriptions of opiates at my office. Greenville probably does about two-thirds of that," boasted Dr. Singer. Interrupting his friend, Doctor C said, "We can triple that. I will give you $5 for every pill 30 mg or less, and $10 for every pill you prescribe over 30 mgs. You can do the math, Doc—an easy ten million every year for your practice. Within twenty-four hours, my brokers can get those pills all over the country, from coast to coast. The sky's the limit here." Dr. Singer raised his last concern: "You can launder all this money through your company, right?" "You got it," said a smiling Doctor C, offering his right hand to Dr. Singer, who quickly took it. That Sunday morning, to Springdale's detriment, a new, more profitable partnership was formed.

Chapter 9: Doctor "C"

ROBERT CHRISTO YANNOPOULOS was an enigma even to his proud first-generation, Greek-American family. His father, Alekos "Christo", was a young man when he arrived in the United States from a small village outside Athens. Alekos opened a successful bakery on the New Jersey shore. He was introduced to his wife, Magda, by anxious Greek friends who wanted their lineage to stay pure. The couple went on to have six children, Robert being the youngest.

Given their long surname, Christo was adopted as the name everyone in the community called the family. In fact Christo's was the name of the bakery that Alekos owned. Long lines quelled up on Saturday for Alekos's famous spinach pies, among other

Greek treasures, such as baklava and moussaka. The bakery was a real family affair, with Magda the silent culinary artist in the kitchen and the ebullient Alekos, or "Alex," schmoozing the customers. All of the children – three girls and three boys – worked in the restaurant, beginning by cleaning tables when they were barely old enough to walk.

But the work ethic developed in the Christo children paid great dividends. As their parents had hoped, their children would not put in long hours running the restaurant as adults. No, the two older Christo children became lawyers – a son and a daughter – and partnered in a successful law firm. Another daughter became a C.P.A. and helped her brother and sister, who opened a burgeoning real estate business selling luxury homes on the New Jersey shore.

That left Robert, "Bobby" Christo Yannopoulos, who broke the family's successful career legacy. The family matriarch, Magda, often blamed herself for his failures, since as the youngest, he did not get the attention she gave the others. No, insisted her husband Alex in his angry days. He had seen signs that his youngest son thought differently than his other children. Alex recalled that Bobby was the only one of his children who would simply disappear from the restaurant

The Girl Who Woke Up in the Morgue

on busy Saturday afternoons. When Alex confronted Bobby later at night, Bobby had no real answer as to why he left, other than saying, "I was bored." His father's infamous paddle, that he rarely had to use on his other children, did not seem to bother Bobby, as he would again simply disappear the following Saturday.

Years later, Bobby's siblings were not as protective toward him as their mother was. Sitting around one of the sibling's large homes during Greek holidays, invariably the family would share "Bobby" stories. Bobby was rarely present during these times, because he was the nomad of the family. He might show up in New Jersey after not contacting anyone for up to a year. The headstrong Bobby did agree to one request that his siblings asked. He called his mother once a month, since they'd convinced him that his anxious mother might die of a heart attack otherwise.

These "Bobby" stories usually occurred after dinner, when the family's bellies were full from Magda's delicious lamb and their dad had gone to the cabinet and poured drinks from his special collection of Ouzo. The discussions would be tinged with both admiration and regret for their missing brother. Their parents recalled that an admiring teacher once said Bobby had tested on the genius level on an aptitude test. However, his intellectual gifts were a double-edged sword. Since studies were easy for Bobby, he just coasted through school. Most nights he hung out with his many friends, who while not bad kids, were more of a rougher crowd. His parents did not care for his unusual choice of friends. They labeled his friends as "KaKa," or bad people, when Bobby took up smoking like them.

Other "Bobby" stories focused on Bobby's great athletic abilities. As a 6'2" runningback on the football field, the chiseled athlete often had to find people to tackle him. Many tacklers opted to bush his legs rather than take a direct hit. With his flowing black hair spilling from his helmet, Bobby's fans took to calling him the "Greek God." Magda often teased her three daughters that Bobby had the best hair in the family. That invariably led to the girls teasing their mother that his thick black curls did not last long, as each time they saw him, more of his dome was exposed.

As usual with "Bobby" stories, these post-dinner family tales ventured toward regret. By his senior year, Bobby had college coaches salivating over his potential. Many saw him as a stud linebacker rather than a runningback, given his penchant for violent contact. He had a fistful of full scholarships that he ultimately rejected.

Bobby told his parents that football was not "fun" anymore. He ended up going to a local New Jersey college that his parents funded. He lasted less than one year there. He spent more time with his neighborhood friends than studying.

Bobby's departure from his home area occurred when he was 20. Always having the gift of gab to go along with his striking image, Bobby sold cars. The job allowed him to sleep late and stay out carousing at night with friends. He liked to gamble, and often visited nearby Atlantic City casinos with a wad of cash. When money got tight, his mother might "lend" him some money from the bakery. He always told her he would pay her the next week, but his understanding mother told him, "Just be a good boy."

One late night at the casino, Bobby met a striking blonde, a young lady with a short dress and long legs. Bobby impressed the girl with the cash he loved to flash with his friends. They started dating. One day, a gentleman approached Bobby's dad, Alex, at the restaurant. A long-time customer of the bakery, the man had decided to talk to Alex before going to the police. His daughter Alexis was seventeen and a senior in high school. She was also pregnant with Bobby's child. The dad wanted to know if Alex's son was going to do the right thing and marry his daughter.

At a Yannopoulos family sit-down later that night, the family confronted Bobby. Magda, always his protector, thought marriage might be good for Bobby. The rest of the family disagreed. To their surprise, Bobby knew that Alexis was only seventeen. He defended himself: "She looks older than me," and blamed the young girl for the situation. "She said she was on the pill." The patriarch of the family exploded at Bobby. "You have disgraced this family. You will do the right thing by this girl. You do not have to marry her, but you will support your child." Bobby looked at his family, took a deep breath and said, "I'm going to the casino." His family sat in stunned silence.

The next day, Bobby got up early and packed a suitcase. The last thing he was going to do with his life was be bogged down with a wife and child. He had been considering this move even before the girl had "tricked" him. Bobby had no desire to remain in New Jersey his whole life. Bobby left his parents' home at 6 a.m. He thought about leaving a note for his mom but decided to call her later. However, the family did not hear from him until a month later.

The Girl Who Woke Up in the Morgue

Fortune smiled on Bobby once at this time – he was going into the nightclub business. Bobby's roommate from his aborted year of college, Jason, came from Ohio. Jason's dad operated a nightclub in Cleveland. An impressed Jason, like many of Bobby's friends, said that his dad could always use good help. Until now, nightclub work had not enticed Bobby.

Bobby was a hit at the Cleveland nightclub from the start. He began as a doorman bouncer, but his imposing physique and glib mind quickly got him management's attention. Soon he was in charge of security for the bustling nightclub. A hidden gem of a venue in the minds of true rock fans, the club engaged both up-and-coming local bands as well as better-known touring bands.

The fast pace, pretty women, and personality-driven aspects of nightclub work appealed to Bobby. Soon Bobby was also participating in the club's management. He helped with advertising, inventory control, and the booking of entertainment. Management especially liked Bobby's intimidating manner as it pertained to staff. Cash reconciliation improved tremendously when Bobby told the bartenders the days of skimming and free drinks were over.

Bobby eagerly learned all the facets of club management. After four years of watching the large amounts of money going in and out of the business, he wanted more and was ready to move on.

He had his eyes on a young band, the Ravens, who periodically played at the club. Whenever they played, the club was overflowing with rabid fans. For the five-member group, their talent had not resonated outside of the Cleveland area. The astute Bobby saw what was missing from these talented musicians – proper management. He saw a group of "knuckleheads" who could play all night but had no ability or desire to market themselves professionally. Bobby became the band's manager and business partner for a 20% fee.

For the majority of the next three years, Bobby was on the road promoting the Ravens. He was a natural marketer and soon secured national prominence for the band. In an effort to secure the Ravens a national record deal, he would arrive early at various record companies with coffee for the administrative staff. He would then use his wily charms on the secretaries to obtain "just five minutes" with their bosses. His persistence and charm eventually paid off. Midnight Records, a major music label, signed the Ravens.

The Girl Who Woke Up in the Morgue

By this time Bobby had made a reputation in the music business and had professional relationships throughout the country. Observing Bobby's special abilities, Midnight Records made Bobby an offer. They offered him a position working for the label as a scout, recruiting and signing bands. For the next ten years, Bobby toured the country for Midnight Records. He was paid handsomely, and as usual with Bobby, he worked hard, both personally and professionally. For a person of Bobby's temperament, the job provided more than monetary rewards. The constant stimulation of new cities, new women, and different casinos fit Bobby perfectly.

After ten years, however, the astute Bobby saw changes in the music landscape. More and more musicians realized that they could get their demo music directly into the hands of producers. Many labels had protocols for direct submission from the artists. Bobby had a colleague in Springdale who had the largest rock nightclub in the area. Bobby thought it might be okay to settle down for a while, and in 2008 he relocated to Springdale. He would no longer be known as Bobby, however. He now introduced himself as "Doctor C."

It was probably inevitable that two ruthless and ambitious personalities would run into each other in Springdale. This was ultimately what happened, to the detriment of the community.

Chapter 10: Kelsey is Released from the Hospital

KELSEY SLOWLY CAME TO UNDERSTAND that she was a minor celebrity in the hospital. She occasionally saw medical personnel pointing at her. Nurses lavished extra attention on her. One asked what "the other side" was like. Her handsome young doctor, Gene Knight, reminded her how lucky she was to have survived this episode.

She was also visited by many people, some her family, and some she did not even know. One day, her mother angrily strode to her bed asking how she could "fucking" do this to herself. Naturally she blamed her "asshole" family for Kelsey's overdose. "When you're released, I'm taking you home." That idea both terrified and comforted Kelsey.

For now, she had no idea what she would do when she was released.

Kelsey's grandmother, Grace Fulton, visited Kelsey once. Grace hovered over her granddaughter protectively and brought her magazines, but Kelsey remembered only her words. "Kelsey, you know the Fulton family has an image to uphold. Family members should not embarrass our name."

One day Kelsey was surprised by an attorney who was able to escape security and introduce himself to her. Attorney John Abbott said that Kelsey had a good legal case to sue the ambulance company, the Medical Examiner's Office, even the funeral director. As he was being led away by security personnel, he dropped his card on her bed.

One day Taylor walked in with the imposing man she had met at the party, "Doctor C." He looked as imposing to Kelsey as she remembered – his bald head so shiny in the hospital lights, he appeared almost angelic. His eyes were not that of an angel, however. They were dark and cold. Taylor barely made eye contact with Kelsey as he mumbled whether she remembered Doctor C. Hardly waiting for an answer to Taylor's question as to how Kelsey felt, Doctor C leaned in close to Kelsey's face. He advised her to fake ignorance if anyone asked where she got the pills that night. He told her to tell them someone might have put them in her drink. Intimidated, Kelsey just nodded. Doctor C abruptly left, and Taylor meekly followed, telling Kelsey he would call her later.

George Fulton also arrived at her bedside, with his cell phone as normal glued to his ear. He sat near Kelsey's legs and rolled his eyes at her, like he wanted to be off the phone, but could not. After the call ended, he asked Kelsey how she was feeling. Kelsey said, "I'm feelin' lucky." George agreed and quickly led into a plan he had developed for her.

George assured her that her apartment and job would be waiting for her when she returned. Kelsey nervously asked, "Returned from where?" After a long sigh, George responded, "You are going into a drug treatment center for at least thirty days." He continued, "You are a lucky girl, and I cannot let my niece become a drug addict." He explained further, "Everything has been arranged. Dr. Knight is on the Board, and I have completed all the paperwork for you to go to the Evergreen Rehabilitation Center here, in Springdale. By the way, don't listen to any of this crap about a lawsuit. We will take care of you." Puzzled by the "we" comment, Kelsey just nodded. George gave Kelsey a quick kiss and left. On his way out, George ran into Dr. Knight. Kelsey, watching through the open door, saw that the two seemed to know each other. She heard her uncle say in an upbeat manner, "She's on board, Gene. As soon as you say she is ready, she will go to Evergreen."

A smiling Dr. Knight entered her room. He looked through a pile of papers that had Kelsey's name on them, and reported that all her organs were functioning well. Initially he was concerned that her heart and lungs, which suffered the greatest shock from her overdose, might have suffered some damage. Looking at her sternly, he said, "Now we want to make sure this never happens again, Kelsey." He cited from her toxicology report that she had consumed several oxycodone pills of considerable strength, perhaps 40 mg each. "The fact that you crushed and inhaled these pills, Kelsey, only added to the danger to you. Never again, right?"

Ashamed, Kelsey could not even look Dr. Knight in the eye. He got up to leave and told her that if her vitals stayed stable for the next forty-eight hours, she would be ready to go to Evergreen.

Alone, lying in her hospital bed, Kelsey had plenty of time to think about her future. She knew she wanted to be an artist one day, her wildest fantasy being that someone would pay her for one of her portraits. She knew that to have any chance of reaching this goal, she needed to go to art school. Drugs had nearly derailed this dream, and a chill went up her spine as for the first time, she experienced how close to death she had come. Her whole life, Kelsey had dreamed of being an artist, having a handsome "soulmate", a crop of children, and the house with the white picket fence. All those dreams had nearly ended because of some small pills that you could find in any medicine cabinet.

Kelsey had to admit that these little pills awakened something in her that was almost indescribable. With them, she was confident and content – not insecure and worried about everything and everyone. With them, there was no past or future, only a euphoric now wherein her body surged with feelings that she was master of the universe. Kelsey hoped that her treatment would help her to master these powerful urges she still felt to consume more pills.

Chapter 11: Kelsey's Treatment at Evergreen

KELSEY WAS RELEASED from the hospital two days after her last meeting with Dr. Knight. She was taken by ambulance to the Evergreen Treatment Center in Springdale. The modern facility resembled a small bank. Kelsey admired the foyer's golden chandelier, upscale Colonial furniture, and distinctive gray rug. She was greeted by the facility's director, Dr. Peggy Schmidt. Smartly attired, the attractive, middle-aged Dr. Schmidt said that she had heard a lot about Kelsey, beyond her notable near-death experience at the funeral home. George Fulton, Kelsey's uncle, was a frequent visitor at the facility. Dr. Schmidt explained that the Fultons had designed and built the Evergreen facility.

The Girl Who Woke Up in the Morgue

Dr. Schmidt gave Kelsey an overview of the Evergreen philosophy. "Its purpose is to care for the medical, emotional, and physical needs of residents in the recovery process," the doctor proudly stated. Kelsey would be at the facility for a minimum of thirty days, which could be extended for up to ninety days. Upon discharge, Kelsey may have to enter a group home, known as a sober house, or receive outpatient treatment, which Evergreen would coordinate.

Dr. Schmidt further explained that Evergreen might have up to twenty-five residents at one time, each having their own room and toilet. Every day was carefully planned between three meals. Residents would participate in individual and group counseling, exercise, vocational training, and arts and crafts.

In Kelsey's first forty-eight hours, the staff's attention would focus on Kelsey's detoxification needs. She would have to provide random urinalysis to their clinic, and to be tested for STDs and any bacterial infections.

Dr. Schmidt asked Kelsey if she had any questions about the program. "Only one," said Kelsey. "How am I going to pay for all of this?" Dr. Schmidt said that Kelsey's health insurance with her employer, the Fulton

Company, would cover all her expenses. This included her physical exams, medications, and outpatient aftercare. Relieved by this news, Kelsey was guided to her private room.

Kelsey was a bit more fortunate in her withdrawal from opiates than others in the facility. On her first night, she heard the hoarse retching and moans of her next-door neighbor. The woman vomited all night, until nothing remained in her stomach. Perhaps Kelsey's nights in the hospital had helped protect her body from this type of physical pain. However, she did experience anxiety and depression in her first forty-eight hours. The facility's physician prescribed buprenorphine for her, which eased her symptoms.

Kelsey quickly eased into a daily schedule, which included meditation and yoga before breakfast. After breakfast, she had individual counseling with her therapist, Linda Green. Counseling sessions were followed by some physical activity. Many residents worked out in the gym, but Kelsey preferred a swim in the facility's pool. Lunch was followed by arts and crafts. Kelsey soon impressed her instructor, Jeremy Small, a retired Springdale art teacher. He said that Kelsey showed real talent, especially with her realistic portraits of others. And then there were the lab tests. Kelsey was surprised at the number of lab tests ordered by Evergreen. Each day she had some type of blood, urine, or saliva screen.

Late afternoons, prior to dinner, was free time for residents. They could read or relax in their rooms, or interact with other residents. Kelsey often played ping-pong in the recreation room during this period. It was there that she met her neighbor, Debbie, who had suffered so much during her first days. Debbie Post, now detoxed, was twenty years old, close to Kelsey's age. She was a pretty, slightly overweight woman with auburn hair and a ready smile. Kelsey soon became aware that Debbie was self-conscious about her missing front tooth. Her frequent smiles prematurely ended in embarrassment.

Kelsey and Debbie became fast friends. Each shared remarkably similar upbringings. Neither had any siblings or had any interactions with their dads. Debbie readily shared with Kelsey that she had been molested as a child by a maternal uncle. "That fucked me up something bad," sighed Debbie with a self-conscious smile, "and my mother took her brother's side." Out of the home by sixteen, Debbie drifted in and out of friends' homes for the past four years. Most of these friends had drug problems. They started with alcohol and marijuana, and quickly moved to prescription pills like Zanex, Percusset, and oxys.

One day over ping-pong, Debbie asked Kelsey how she got addicted. Kelsey recoiled, as up until then she did not consider herself an addict. "I just did some pills with my boyfriend. I guess they were too strong, and I was resuscitated in a funeral home." Debbie laughed so hard, she didn't even worry about the gap in her smile. "Boy, that's a good one. Look, I started by taking pills with my boyfriend too, but I soon graduated to heroin." Kelsey shook her head. "I would never do heroin." "Yeah, me too, but once you feel that silk in your bones, you're hooked. Every time I relapse, I remember the feeling of the first hit of heroin. It's magical."

Kelsey asked, "You've been to treatment before?" "Yeah, I'm not even from around here. I'm from Coolidge, two hundred miles away. I was in two separate facilities in Coolidge." "How did you end up in Springdale?" asked Kelsey. "Someone helped me get here. This was the only facility that would take me. It's an insurance thing, I guess. Three strikes and I'm out, right, Kelsey?" said a tight-lipped Debbie. "No," said Kelsey, "we will both get better." "Sure." "Oh, my game," yelled Debbie as she slammed the ball over the net.

The Girl Who Woke Up in the Morgue

Kelsey looked forward to her therapy sessions with Dr. Green. She had learned that Linda Green was a recovering addict. Sober for seven years, Dr. Green now devoted her life to helping others avoid some of the mistakes she had made. And more importantly, she helped people to understand why they needed the drugs. Starting at age sixteen, Linda had experienced years of addiction, interspersed with a roller-coaster pattern of recovery and relapse. Linda told Kelsey that she got clean at age twenty-three and turned her life around. Now thirty, in the last seven years, she had earned her college degree, gotten married, and had two healthy children, ages four and two. "I'm still an addict," said Linda to Kelsey, "but one who consciously chooses not to consume drugs. I had to learn to love myself before I could make that choice." As she intensely looked deep into Kelsey's eyes, she asked, "Are you ready to try to understand what you were escaping from with drugs?"

Kelsey closed her eyes at Dr. Green's invitation. "I hate myself. I've been a burden to everyone since I was born. Why would anyone love me, anyway? I can't do anything."

"Okay, Kelsey, one issue at a time. Obviously you don't feel good about yourself. My reaction is, why do you accept all the burden about your supposed failures? Is it possible a lot of people have let you down in your young life?" Silent, Kelsey buried her face in her hands.

Dr. Green asked, "Tell me about your parents." Kelsey said, "I don't see my mom right now. She lives in Oxford with her boyfriend, but she has raised me most of my life."

"And your dad?" said Dr. Green. "They were both eighteen when they had me. He never really wanted a child. I have not seen him in years. But from what I hear, he was a pretty good artist. I heard he does tattoos now. I guess that's all I got from him. My mom always called him 'a fucking loser', pardon my language."

Dr. Green asked, "Is that how your mother always talked about him?" Kelsey retorted, "Him? She calls everyone a fucking loser – her boyfriends, her mother, her brothers, whoever. Anyone who gets her mad is a loser."

"It sounds like she is an angry woman. Kelsey defended her mom, "It hasn't been easy for her, having me at a young age, and raising me by herself." Dr. Green asked, "Do you feel responsible for your mother's anger, Kelsey?" Without looking up, Kelsey nodded.

Dr. Green said sternly, "Kelsey, look at me." Kelsey listened as Dr. Green spoke. "I

The Girl Who Woke Up in the Morgue

don't know you well yet, but I can tell you are a good person whose normal reflex is to blame yourself, even when it's a shitty reality that has affected you. If you want, I'll help you confront some of your demons – some forced upon you, and some you brought on yourself. My goal is to help you unlock the real Kelsey, to examine all your fears, to grieve all your losses, and most importantly, to convince you to view yourself as a worthy contributor to your world. Are you ready to accept this challenge over the next weeks, as we work together?" Kelsey, feeling a touch less alienated than normal, said, "Yes."

Kelsey did just that, meeting Linda Green three times per week in the following days. Layer by layer, Linda helped Kelsey to understand just who she was. They examined Kelsey's childhood, the abandonment by her dad, and the difficult nature of her mom. They examined her relationship with her extended family, the Fultons, and her devalued sense of self with them. Most importantly, they explored what drugs provided to Kelsey and what they replaced in her psyche. Slowly, Kelsey articulated a vision for herself that included art as a career, and a family life with someone far better than her own.

Kelsey also truly looked forward to the group therapy sessions, which occurred each night. They were led by a dynamic leader, Dr. Sherri Carlson, a psychologist who specialized in addiction recovery. Every night, up to twenty residents shared their difficult paths to addiction. Kelsey was tremendously moved by these narratives as she realized she was not alone in her recovery. She listened as many good people told of the bad things they had done because of this terrible addiction.

Dr. Carlson explained a little of the history of opioid drugs. Made from the opium poppy plant, they are a class of drugs designed to help relieve pain. The first opioid morphine was created in 1803. In the late 1990s, scientists were able to replicate the chemical structure of the poppy plant. By the turn of this century, synthetic drugs could be inexpensively mass produced. Opioids such as hydrocodone, Vicodin, OxyContin, and Zanax quickly found their way into America's medicine cabinets.

She helped the group to understand the science behind opioid addiction as she talked about how these drugs were designed to release endorphins. She explained how these "feel-good" receptors are wired to attach to the pleasure center of the brain. The group members shared their first euphoric feelings on these pills. The residents used adjectives like "all powerful", "heaven like", and "indescribable pleasure" to describe their first experiences. Many residents shared that they felt addicted from their very first pill. Others said it took up to a month.

Remarkably, all the residents quickly felt an uncontrollable urge to use pills. Despite all the negative consequences that soon coalesced – shame, stealing from parents and friends – they all wanted to recapture the intensity of that first high.

Invariably their cravings for opioids quickly went from experiencing a high to not suffering a withdrawal. Every morning, their mission upon awakening was not washing up or getting a coffee. No, their immediate mission was to get pills – enough so that their bodies would not ache. Kelsey listened as her group members described intense physical symptoms such as nausea, constipation, and body aches, as well as emotional responses such as anxiety and irritability and depression. To prevent these symptoms, the addicts needed more and more opioids in their bodies. Relationships, careers, and dreams immediately fell victim to the pursuit of more drugs.

During these group sessions, Kelsey observed that several faces looked vaguely familiar. During a coffee break, she approached one such person, named Peter. Instantly, he recognized her as Taylor's girlfriend. He explained that Taylor used to be his source for drugs on the street. He had not approached her earlier because he was with her the night she overdosed. "I was at the party," said Peter. He introduced her to another resident named Andrea, who also looked familiar to Kelsey. Andrea explained that she'd once dated "Doctor C", who Kelsey remembered from the party.

Over the next thirty days, Kelsey developed relationships with other residents of Evergreen. Her favorite activity was drawing portraits of her new friends as gifts to them. Kelsey had to use a bit of positive imagination for some of the portraits, to imagine her subjects in a healthier state. For example, with her friend Debbie, she was careful to add a full set of teeth to her smiling visage. Many residents appeared almost gaunt, their clothes nearly falling off their thin frames. While some residents started to physically reflect their overall positive care from Evergreen, most bore the effects of detoxification in their sad eyes.

Before she knew it, Kelsey realized that her sixty days at Evergreen were over. Uplifted by her therapy and friendships, Kelsey wanted to stay another sixty days. She felt a confidence growing within her, a confidence that she was a good person.

The Girl Who Woke Up in the Morgue

Linda Green, her individual therapist, observed her positive growth. She also supported Kelsey's desire to remain at Evergreen and knew it would help to ensure she didn't relapse. Unfortunately, after sixty days, Dr. Peggy Schmidt told Kelsey that her insurance would not pay for further residential treatment at Evergreen. However, it would pay for a sober halfway house. Consequently, soon Kelsey was on her way to the Spring Valley Sober House in Springdale.

Chapter 12:
More Springdale Deaths

IN THE WEEKS FOLLOWING Kelsey's miracle awakening, Sonny Fiorentino had three more overdose deaths. He had the unfortunate experience as a funeral director of burying Springdale's youth, rather than its elderly. Two of the youths were in their teens, and one person was in his early twenties. This was a new frontier for Sonny, as occasionally – perhaps once every two or three years - he might bury a youth from a car accident, or even more rarely, from cancer. Since the calendar had turned to 2010, he had buried six young people from drug overdoses.

Sonny understood that the public held many myths about the job of a funeral director. One of which was that most of his work was with the dead more than the living. In fact, the majority of Sonny's work was with grief-troubled families who did not want to be in a funeral home. Administrative tasks such as acquiring death certificates and burial permits require considerable time with family members. More importantly, families often relied on him for guidance about suitable and profound services for a loved one. Like his grandfather and his father, Sonny took a patient approach to helping a family choose services that had unique meaning – whether that involved religious service or not.

These interactions, with families burying the young who were supposed to outlive the older family members who met with Sonny, were extremely emotional. A disturbing trend revealed itself in these three overdose deaths. Each family had no suspicion that their loved one had a serious drug issue – never mind that they would die from it.

With one family, their son was a star football player who suffered a back injury during a game. Their doctor had prescribed a pain medication and assured them that these pills were harmless. Reassured that pills coming from a pharmacy could not be addictive, this family thought they were helping their son get back on the football field. While they gradually witnessed some behavioral changes in their son – especially irritability when he ran out of pills – their doctor reassured them that this was normal. The doctor was not even worried when their son's pills were all used up by their son weeks before they should have been. He was found in a known drug house. His toxicology report listed heroin as the cause of death.

With the second overdose family, their loved one was a young lady in her twenties who had anxiety and depression issues. During a brief hospitalization for related stomachaches, a psychiatrist had prescribed medication for her mood disorder. The medication was designed to stimulate or elevate the girl's behavior. Again, the family did not fear any addictive issues with the prescribed pills. The parents told Sonny that they immediately saw dramatic changes in their daughter. Initially she seemed better, but she grew so dependent on her new euphoria that the prescriptions ran out seemingly overnight. In response, her doctor ordered more pills to counter the initial ones. These were designed to sedate her from the effects of the first pills. Her parents watched as their daughter went from near mania to sleeping for days. One day, she went to sleep and did not wake up. Her prescription bottle was found next to her cold hands.

The Girl Who Woke Up in the Morgue

With the third person Sonny buried, the decedent, a nineteen-year-old male, had been in a serious car accident and was hospitalized for several weeks. To control his serious pain, the individual was kept pain-free with considerable amounts of OxyContin, a stronger version of Oxycodone. Upon his discharge, the youth's family saw dramatic changes in his behavior. He constantly told his parents he was in pain and could not wait the six hours for the next pill. He threatened his family that if he did not get the pills, he would get them on the "street." His family told the doctor, who simply increased the strength of his pills from 30 mg to 60 mg.

Sonny learned that the common thread with the three families was the quickness of their loved ones' apparent addiction to pain medication. They saw noticeable irritability when their loved ones' medication wore off. They were constantly seeking more pills, and often stole from their parents to buy pills on the street. Each of these families, while worried about the rapid deterioration of their loved one, did not see death occurring. What they later learned from toxicology results was their loved ones soon turned to the streets for even stronger drugs. One of the young men's death certificates listed heroin as the cause of death.

Stephen Rocco

One Saturday, Sonny was sitting in his office contemplating the sad events occurring in Springdale. He pondered whether other young folks were dying from this scourge in other communities. His thoughts were interrupted by a call on his business line. The call was from Bob Fischer, a close friend who owned a hardware store in Springdale. His voice almost unrecognizable, Bob said that his son, Robert Junior, had been found dead that morning. Afraid to even ask Bob about the circumstances of the death, Sonny feared another drug casualty. He knew that Robert Junior had graduated from Springdale High School a few years ago. Bob Fischer asked Sonny, "Can you come here? My wife is a mess."

"Of course, I'll be right there."

Sonny could hear the wails emanating from the Fischer home as he got out of his car. This was one time he wished his great-grandfather had opened any other business but a funeral home. Sonny offered his condolences to the stunned family members, who had quickly gathered in the home. Recognizing Mrs. Fischer, Sonny hugged her and whispered, "I'll take care of your son."

Mrs. Fischer ushered Sonny into the nearby kitchen and asked him, "What happens now?" Sonny, having already called the

The Girl Who Woke Up in the Morgue

Medical Examiner's Office, told her that Robert Junior would be examined over the next forty-eight hours. "I will then pick up your son, and we can plan his services."

Mr. Fischer buried his head in his hands and said that his son, known as "Junior," now age twenty, worked with him in the hardware store. He told Sonny that Junior was a model son, who never gave him an ounce of trouble. Sonny simply listened as his friend relayed that about six months ago, Junior had joined a new set of friends. He had played guitar in the high school orchestra, and also joined a band after high school on days he was not working. Junior hung out with his bandmates, practicing with them several times a week. Mr. Fischer mentioned with pride that Junior and his band had performed at a Springdale Fourth of July community event. But Mr. Fischer also shared his and his wife's concerns that Junior's bandmates were a bit older and a bit "worldly" for their son, who was a rather shy. Junior did seem to come out of his shell with them, and was protective of his new friends, often saying to his dad, "You worry too much." "But," said Mr. Fischer, "the sad truth is, I did not worry enough about these people." Sonny knew enough not to ask his friend any more about this comment.

In the next few days, Sonny picked up Junior and planned funeral services with the Fischer family. The family had planned a wake service one night, church services the next morning, and burial at Springdale Cemetery. The medical examiner had not determined the cause of death yet, to the chagrin of the Fischer family.

The night of the wake was as difficult for Sonny as any other death he had serviced. The sight of her son's handsome young face in the white casket was too much for Mrs. Fischer. She collapsed on top of him as Mr. Fischer tearfully tried to pry her away. The family carefully placed Junior's ever-present guitar beside him in the casket.

The members of the Springdale community poured into the funeral home to console the popular Fischer family and pay their respects to Robert Junior The reverence for this sacred time was disturbed by some people in Sonny's parking lot adjacent to the funeral home. Sonny's staff told him that a group of young people in jeans and leather vests had gathered there during the wake, smoking marijuana and drinking shots. Sonny questioned the group. "Are you friends of the Fischers?" Of the five individuals, only one made eye contact with Sonny. His eyes were glazed and obviously high on something as he

The Girl Who Woke Up in the Morgue

responded, "We're cool." An angry Sonny snapped, "This is not cool. My friend is burying his son. I think you had better leave the premises." One of the quiet members, whose face was covered with long blonde hair, said, "We loved Bobby. We were in a band with him. We are just having a toast to him." Sonny surprised himself and did not address the blame issue. "I want you to leave now. My staff will give a ride to any of you who need it. If you're not in better shape tomorrow, I don't think you should go to Bobby's funeral. His family is upset with some of you." As Sonny watched, the group wordlessly left the parking lot.

As the wake was ending, Sonny's staff told him there was another disturbance in one of the bathrooms. Sonny entered the bathroom and found about eight noisy people, some of the same folks who had been drinking and smoking in his parking lot.

One person was inhaling a substance that appeared to be crushed near the sink. The other individuals appeared glassy-eyed, and some were actually laughing. Sonny ordered them out of the bathroom, and in a disgusted tone, he admonished them. "Your friend is lying in a casket upstairs, and this is how you pay your respects to him?" The group left the funeral home, and Sonny made sure the Fischers did not hear of this episode.

That night, before the Fischer boy's burial the next morning, Sonny brooded alone in his expansive apartment above the funeral home. He had sat with more and more bereaved families who told them what a great kid Sonny was burying. Universally, all of the families had told him their child's addiction occurred almost overnight. How could these kids be doing drugs in the same funeral home where their friend was lifeless and lying in a casket? Unable to sleep, Sonny poured himself a whiskey as he contemplated all these young deaths. How strong were these drugs? Sonny and his family had occasionally buried drug overdose victims over the years. Those victims normally had a long-standing history of drug use, and their families were well aware and often tried to aid their recovery. He sighed to himself. "But these recent families didn't even get a chance to help their loved ones; these addictions do not afford second chances."

Sonny made a promise that night that he could ignore this problem no longer. He loved Springdale and its people too much to see it ravaged by a problem apparent only to the bereaved. Still angry about the incident in the funeral home, he wrote a message for the youths who would return in the morning.

The Girl Who Woke Up in the Morgue

Pouring himself another whiskey, he wrote a poem – something he had never done in his life. The anguish he felt for all the people he had serviced due to drugs seemed to flow into his pen, and in fifteen minutes he wrote…

A Funeral Director's Wish
I wish you could see
What your late brethren have taught me
No decisions are left
Shame and regret no more

I wish you could listen
To the guilt and anguish
That is your legacy
An eternal weight on those left behind

I wish you could hear
The echoes of your death
"So much to offer"
"So much to love"

I wish you were me
Learning lessons from fateful decisions
Of choosing to embrace a high,
Left
A world denied your talents

Early the next morning, Mr. and Mrs. Fischer returned to Sonny's funeral home to do something no parent ever wants to do –

bury their child. Sonny was happy to see that Bobby J's bandmates did not attend the morning service. Probably not even up yet, Sonny thought to himself. At the same time this funeral resonated to Sonny that there was a whole young population of drug-damaged souls in his beloved Springdale. Early, before the service, Sonny had showed Bob Fischer the poem he had written. Bob hugged Sonny and asked him to read it to the congregation at Junior's church service. Bob said, "If it helps just one person, Sonny, it would be a fitting legacy for my wonderful son." Sonny did read the poem as a eulogy for Junior, and by the last line, tears were welling in Sonny's eyes.

Chapter 13: Another Opiate Funeral

SONNY FIORENTINO WAS ANGRY. It was late summer 2010, and he had buried another of Springdale's youths today. He'd witnessed a common phenomenon that the country was observing. This particular young man, Sam Carlson, age eighteen, had died of a heroin overdose. His distraught family could not believe that they were planning their teenager's funeral. Up until three months ago, Sam was the model son that other parents used to motivate their own children. He was an honor roll student, popular star athlete, and vice president of his graduation class.

The Carsons sadly told Sam's story to Sonny… In March of his senior year, soon after being accepted to his top college choice, Sam had an emergency appendectomy. He was prescribed a thirty-day prescription of pain medication. Apparently Sam got hooked immediately, but his parents, Fred and Marcia Carson, were oblivious to his descent. In April they saw some slight changes in their son. By May they started to worry about these growing personality changes. Sam became sullen and withdrawn. He punched a hole in his bedroom wall. When his physician would not renew his pain medication, Sam stole money from his mother's purse, and later the Carsons found out that he'd sold his laptop.

Sam later apologized profusely to his mom, tearfully reassuring her that he was fine. But in late May, his behavior worsened. He left the Carson home early in the morning and returned at night, his eyes glazed. His appearance, which had defined him as one of Springdale High's "best dressed," deteriorated - as he often wore the same clothes for days. Sam refused to return the calls of his many friends and began spending time with people the Carsons had never seen.

By early June, the Carson's could no longer ignore their growing concerns. They held a mini-intervention with Sam's younger siblings at the family home. It was then that Sam confessed he was consuming pain medication he'd gotten on the street. Stunned, the Carsons learned from Sam that he now had

The Girl Who Woke Up in the Morgue

a desperate need for more and stronger medication. In fact, during the intervention, Sam abruptly left, saying that he needed to get some pills or he would be physically sick. His parents begged him to stay and promised to take him to the hospital. But he ran through their arms and did not return for two days.

Sonny listened as the Carsons jumped into a desperate mission to save Sam's life. Marcia recalled yelling at Sam's surgeon, who'd never warned them about the risk associated with these pills. Angrily, Fred Carson said that the doctor's response was to tell them to bring Sam into him. The doctor would then prescribe a lower dosage of pills and "wean" Sam from them. The doctor insisted that these pills were not addictive.

However, the Carsons did not believe that. The rapid changes they witnessed in Sam – both physical and emotional – convinced the Carsons that Sam required intense treatment. Consulting with law enforcement and drug experts, Fred realized his son needed to be in a residential treatment facility. The parents arranged for their son to get a placement at the Evergreen facility. Fortunately, Mr. Carson was informed that his comprehensive medical insurance would cover Sam's treatment for up to ninety days.

On Friday, June 16, the Carson family had their last intervention with their son. He begged for forgiveness and consented to go into treatment. He was tired of feeling sick, and disclosed that he now used drugs more to prevent withdrawal symptoms than to get high. "I want you to be proud of me again," he told his parents. These were the last words Sam's parents heard from their son. Sometime later that night, Sam got out of bed and went out to purchase more pills.

When the stunned Carsons were making funeral arrangements with Sonny, they originally wanted private services for their popular son. Fred Carson feared the stigma of a "junkie" death from the community. Sonny surprised himself in his response to the grieving father; "God does not make junk." Sonny had first heard those words in a eulogy offered by a recovered addict burying her friend. Sonny helped the Carsons see that the Springdale community needed to come together to grieve, and to support the Carson family with collective arms for their beloved son.

The wake service for Sam Carson was one of the largest Sonny had ever seen. Tearful classmates waited up to three hours to pay their final respects to their friend Sam. They seemed in disbelief that one of their own age could die. Outside the chapel, Sonny heard community members in small groups voicing concern about these young deaths. Some seemed to blame the victims. He overheard one parent say, "That would never happen to my kid." Sonny had to say something. He approached the man and commented, "Don't be so sure. These drugs are insidious and can capture anyone in their path." Surprised, the man did not immediately respond, but then predicted with a silent laugh, "I won't bury anyone in my family."

Later, when Sonny obtained Sam's death certificate for the Carson family, he observed a secondary cause of death beyond heroin. It seemed that the heroin Sam ingested had been laced with fentanyl. Sonny had not heard of this drug before. Intrigued, he did some research. To his horror he learned that this newer synthetic opiate was up to one hundred times more powerful than morphine. It was designed to treat only end-stage patients in severe pain. Sonny learned that the dealers were now adding this drug to heroin, and some sold pills with fentanyl. His quest to solve this plague in Springdale took on a new urgency. "I'm going to call Skip. Maybe we can come up with a plan to save our community," Sonny thought.

Chapter 14:
Detective Skip LeBlanc

TYPICALLY, DETECTIVE LEBLANC did not shave on weekends. On this Saturday, however, he had a special meeting so he found himself looking at his mug in the mirror. Now 48, he had more than a speck of gray in his thinning hair, and more gray than brown in the combination mustache and beard that surrounded his mouth.

Drying his face, he heard his wife June enter the bedroom. "What are the kids up to today?" Skip asked his wife. "Oh, the usual; soccer practice for both of them, and then I'll drive them all over town to see their friends." Skip laughed, "Well, Kevin is going to have his learner's permit next year. I don't know if that's good or bad." June sighed, "The years are flying by. We will be visiting colleges before we know it."

Skip checked his face in the mirror, since he was prone to miss spots as he detested shaving. He thought to himself, as long as Chief Powell is in, I'll never be able to have a full beard. Chief Powell was Springdale's longtime law-and-order chief of police. Skip had to admit that although the chief resisted change in a changing world, he had been good to him. He had made Skip a detective in 2005, and five years later, he was the lead detective in Springdale. He led a small department with two other detectives. Chief Powell said that Skip did not need more detectives, because Springdale did not have much major crime like nearby cities did. Skip LeBlanc was not so sure.

Skip gave a brief kiss to June, telling her that he had a meeting with Sonny Fiorentino at the funeral home. "Tell him I said hello. I can't believe Sonny never got married. Lots of girls in high school wanted to date him." Skip said, "I don't know. I think his father dying so young threw him for a loop. It's like he married the business." "Too bad," said June, "all alone in that building."

Driving to the meeting with Sonny, Skip contemplated how life had turned out pretty good for himself. He and June had two children--Jayson, age 15, and Emma, age 13. The children seemed happy, enjoyed hanging with their parents, and had plenty of friends. Jayson was a sophomore at Springdale High School, and Emma was an eighth-grade student at the middle school. They say girls could be tough, thought Skip, but Emma was unselfish to a fault. She was the one that her group of friends relied on to help them solve their problems. Jayson was the star pitcher on the junior varsity baseball team and the athlete Skip wished he had been at Springdale High thirty years ago.

Skip and June were classmates who graduated from Springdale High in 1980. We have a thirty-year reunion coming up this year, thought an incredulous Skip. He and June started dating in their junior year of high school, and aside from his four years in the military, had never been apart. Each of them loved Springdale and saw no reason not to raise their children there. Many in their social circle had been friends since high school.

Skip had wanted to be a police officer for as long as he could remember. He had admired the shiny cars and polished uniforms of police officers since he was a young boy. As he got older, Skip admired the respect that good police officers earned. Skip recalled on Senior Night in high school, he and his friends were caught drinking in one of Springdale's parks. The officer, who was a friend of Skip's dad, confiscated all the youths' car keys and told them to go to the station in the morning to retrieve them. He let them continue drinking their beer but warned them to "Keep the noise down." Skip had never forgotten that lesson. He viewed law enforcement as community service and always dug a bit deeper to understand wayward individuals. Some of his best professional days were lecturing Springdale students. He wanted them to be vigilant about being agents for good, rather than bad. Skip relayed one important lesson to students about what criminals had taught him. Most had a profound sense of regret that they'd chosen the wrong way when confronted with life's choices.

Skip drove up the massive driveway of the Fiorentino Funeral Home. Sonny had three funerals earlier that Saturday morning, so the funeral home was a buzz of activity. Staff were cleaning up flowers from the chapel; others were vacuuming the several limousines in the garage. One of the female staff looked vaguely familiar to Skip, but he could not place where he had met her.

He was soon greeted by the smiling face of his friend Sonny Fiorentino. "Does that young lady look familiar?" asked Sonny. "I was just thinking that very thing, Sonny. Who is she?" "That's the girl we saved, who woke up in the funeral home." Turning to Kelsey, Sonny called her over to them. "Kelsey, this is my friend from high school, Detective Skip LeBlanc. He was at your apartment the night of your accident." Kelsey smiled warmly, "I want to thank you. I know I was lucky to survive that night. I'm working hard on my recovery."

Skip smiled back warmly. This was just the type of interaction that helped maintain his passion for the job. Sonny said, "Kelsey, if you can before you go to your meeting, can you gas up the cars for Monday?" Kelsey amiably responded, "Sure."

Sonny had called this meeting with Skip after his meeting with the Springdale funeral directors. Skip readily agreed to the meeting, because he had the same concerns over the drugs as Sonny. They agreed that beneath the surface of their bucolic town of Springdale, a percolating abuse of legal drugs was ensnaring more and more people.

Sonny told Skip about the number of drug deaths they had counted – eight in the last six months, including Mrs. Nelson. Sonny asked if this problem was on the police department's radar. Skip replied, "That's what I cannot understand. I tried to start an investigation, but the chief called it "a waste of time." Chief Powell said that the drugs "are only getting the bad kids, who abuse the drugs." Skip got the sense that the chief felt these drugs had a useful value – weeding out Springdale's bad element. Skip said that even when he brought evidence to Chief Powell proving that the problem was exploding, the chief had dismissed it. He explained that paramedics were averaging five overdose calls each weekend. "If not for the Narcan," said Skip, "you would have a lot more business." Skip revealed that frustrated recovery teams were resuscitating some of the same kids over and over again.

Sonny relayed to Skip the recent meeting he'd had with Dr. Jerome Singer. Skip shook his frustrated head as he heard the doctor's argument that these pills were not addictive. An angry Skip said, "That's the damn problem. People don't see that these pills found in medicine cabinets are really poison." Skip instantly recalled an incident that occurred with his son Jayson at middle school. Jayson's young classmate had two pain pills that he had taken from his mother and wanted to share them with Jayson. A frightened Jayson had asked his father, "What do these pills do?" Skip recalled that even he didn't take the issue seriously at the time.

Skip and Sonny soon came to the conclusion that a growing menace was in their midst. Sonny said, "We need to find out where all these pills are coming from." "I can call in some federal agencies, like the DEA," said Skip, "But I've got to get more information. I can't go over my boss's head without more evidence."

A bit frustrated, both men agreed to stay in close touch with one another. Skip said that he would encourage his detectives to build informants. Sonny would be a bit more inquisitive toward the people coming into his funeral home. The friends of the young drug victims knew where the drugs were coming from.

Chapter 15: Pharmaceutical Greed

"WHEN'S OUR NEXT TRIP, ROB? I'm getting a bit bored." Dr. Singer smiled at the young pharmaceutical salesman in his office. Rob was short for Robert McNulty, who was the top salesman for the Omnifix Medical Company. Dr. Singer had known Rob now for seven years. Profit was the basis of the relationship.

In the go-go days of the opiate onslaught in America, Dr. Singer's office was literally assaulted by opiate salespeople like Rob. Each representative touted the unique benefit of their drugs. More importantly, they literally fought over one another to offer benefits to Dr. Singer and others like him. Luxury trips to the Cayman Islands, his-and-her Rolex watches, and generous "speaker fees" were among the benefits offered to Dr. Singer. The amount of the "speaker fees" was based on the volume of opiates he sold. The "speaking" was simply sharing a cocktail with medical colleagues while convincing them to use a particular drug company.

Dr. Singer recalled that he had met Rob McNulty around 2003. The handsome, former quarterback made an impression on most people with his enthusiastic ardor. He was loud, with an engaging personality that left most people smiling. Dr. Singer, like most physicians, loved to hear of Rob's exploits on the football field.

Following a devastating knee injury early in his junior year, Rob dropped out of college. Never a great student, he could no longer rely on coeds to do his assignments. They had quickly moved on to the new quarterback. So Rob began working in a series of jobs that relied on his charming personal skills. He was a personal trainer but was eventually asked to leave the gym because of the trouble he caused with his married female clients. He became a bartender, then a car salesman. But nothing seemed to be the right "fit".

In 2000, Rob saw a help wanted advertisement from a new pharmaceutical company called Omnifix. Rob learned that a new class of safe pain medications known as

The Girl Who Woke Up in the Morgue

opiates had been developed in the past decade, and Omnifix was involved in their sales and distribution. Essentially the medication was the same from company to company. One company's Dilaudid, Percocet, or Vicodin was the same as the others.

Rob was hired, and the athlete in him soon grew excited as he listened to his bosses at Omnifix compare their goals to an athletic competition. "Your goal is to out-hustle the competition," they repeated over and over at sales meetings, and the phrase soon became Rob's mantra. He immersed himself in the litany of drugs produced by his company. Soon, Rob became as comfortable discussing the differences between hydrocodone and oxycodone as he'd once been calling football plays. He learned one other lesson: "Find your Orca." For a sales rep, an Orca was a doctor who wanted to sell as many pain pills as Rob did.

Rob was a natural in this new business. Normally he charmed the office secretaries with flowers and flattery. He looked at the dour faces of the other pharmaceutical salespeople he met in the office, probing him to be even more effusive. The secretaries smiled at his football stories and ushered him into their bosses' offices before his longer-waiting colleagues.

Stephen Rocco

It did not take Rob long to charm Dr. Singer. The doctor loved to hear Rob's football stories but was especially excited to hear about his sexual conquests with the cheerleaders. Their long talks in his office had Dr. Singer reflecting on the type of college experience he'd missed out on because of his constant need to study. Deep in Dr. Singer's consciousness were the memories of the shy, non-athletic youth who never knew what to say to girls.

In those early years, the relationship between Rob and Dr. Singer strengthened. They were bonded through business trips taken by the two men, as Dr. Singer's wife, Marcia, was busy raising the couple's two young children. Rob's bosses allowed an unheard-of $25,000 speaker fee for Dr. Singer. After the doctor's divorce, Rob made sure that a bevy of bikini-clad ladies paid special attention to Dr. Singer on these trips.

By 2008, Rob could not believe his good fortune. He had found his "Orca". Dr. Singer was as ambitious to be rich as the salesman himself. Also by this time, the doctor had five other physicians in his offices with the same mindset. Rob was the highest earning representative at Omnifix, earning nearly a million dollars a year. He was on top of the world, and he rarely contemplated the "might

The Girl Who Woke Up in the Morgue

have been" of his football career as he once did. His new lakeside condo was seemingly occupied by new girlfriends each night, to the point that Rob often forgot their names by morning.

"I'm getting bored," repeated a smiling Dr. Singer to his young friend. One day, Rob did not respond with his normal loud laugh. "Have you heard about any new regulation on the pain medications?" he asked. In fact, as it was 2009, Dr. Singer had read some professional literature indicating that some patients responded negatively to the drugs. "No," replied Dr. Singer, employing his classic denial. "Oh and by the way, I want to thank you for introducing me to Andrea last week. My legs are heavy this morning, if you know what I mean." "No problem," said Rob, who tried to smile but was distracted. Although his normal philosophy was to mirror the demeanor of the buyer, he could not use this approach today. "I just left a meeting at Omnifix," he told the doctor. "They are worried that the government is going to regulate these medications. They are concerned that some young people are dying when they abuse the pills."

"That's right," said Dr. Singer. "It's the abuse of these pills that is the problem. We have had these pills, what, about ten years now?" Rob nodded. "Well," continued Dr. Singer, "If there were problems, we would have discovered them by now. I think your company is overreacting. The drugs do much more good than bad. My patients out there have never felt better. Besides, the kids that are dying had problems anyway."

With Dr. Singer's coaching, Rob felt a bit better. He smiled and said, "Maybe we can rent the yacht this weekend." "Great," said Dr. Singer. " I was supposed to have the kids this weekend, but that's not a problem. Do you think you can invite the girl Andrea again?" "Sure," said Rob with nearly his normal enthusiasm. "We will have a great time." "Oh," said Dr. Singer, "and can I invite a couple of the pharmacists?"

Both Doctor C and Dr. Singer had cultivated a group of like-minded pharmacists to dispense the prescriptions. These pharmacists did not question the amount of pills, nor their strength. Dr. Singer routinely ordered up to one hundred pills for a normal prescription, with at least 50mg in strength. Doctor C could charge up to $50 to $75 on the street for each of these strong pills.

Feeling better after Dr. Singer's pep talk, Rob left the office in recovered spirits. "See you this weekend, Doc, normal time at the dock." "Great, and I'll see Andrea?"

The Girl Who Woke Up in the Morgue

"Naturally," said a smiling Rob as he waved goodbye. As Rob walked into the outer office, Dr. Singer smiled when he heard his flirtatious receptionist thank Rob for the lovely flowers.

Dr. Singer's smile quickly disappeared as he immersed himself into his new business. "Have those rehab checks come in from the insurance company on the Fielder woman, Delores?" "Not yet," responded Delores. "That insurance company is slow. But I did get the SSDI check for Mr. Davis, who just left Evergreen. He is going into the sober house today." "Ok,ay great, thank you." So consumed was Dr. Singer in this rehabilitation business that he'd moved his most competent administrator, Delores St. Gelais, solely into this area. The older woman had also been a long-time secretary to his dad, and the younger Dr. Singer had to constantly discourage her from retiring.

Dr. Singer had not been completely honest with Rob McNulty. The prescient doctor did see opiate problems on the horizon. While he still believed the drugs to be safe, he knew the government now had some concerns. As Dr. Singer continued to blame patients for abusing the drugs, he knew that some of his colleagues thought differently. They were very concerned that the drugs were addictive. By 2008, some states had passed mild regulations monitoring the opiate levels that could be issued by state doctors. "These regulations will only grow more restrictive in the future," thought Dr. Singer. One state had even limited prescriptions to only three days' worth of medication.

Dr. Singer also had growing concern about his partnership with Doctor C. He had learned that his partner had coerced some elderly physicians in a nearby town to literally sell their prescription books with their signatures to Doctor C. Then, Doctor C. would simply fill out the prescriptions and have his dealers fill them naturally at maximum levels of pills. Dr. Singer blamed this practice on the recent spate of deaths in the Springdale area, displaying his classic denial about his own role in these schemes.

So Dr. Singer decided to enter into the drug rehabilitation business, which was a much cleaner venture with a profitable future. In 2007, he called his friends, the Fultons, and had them design a state-of-the-art treatment facility. The Evergreen facility soon drew patients from all over the country. For Dr. Singer, the most important requirement was that the residents have insurance, preferably private insurance. Sure, he took some patients who self-paid, but few could afford his $2000 a day rate. Private insurance companies did not quibble over the price, and if the doctor got lucky, the resident would get a ninety-day placement.

Public insurers such as Medicaid or SSDI paid about fifty percent of the private rate. Dr. Singer's reluctance to accept the discount was eased because the government checks came in like clockwork – the first of every month.

Realizing the full potential of this treatment racket, Dr. Singer bought two rundown homes in Springdale neighborhoods and turned them into sober houses. These homes served as the next phase of treatment for patients released from Evergreen. Again, he called his friends the Fultons to help renovate the homes. But these renovations were not like the palatial Evergreen facility. The Fultons were told to maximize the occupancy in each bedroom and minimize any other costs.

While Dr. Singer did not actively try to re-addict patients in these homes, it was almost inevitable, given their locations. Residents going to work from the Spring Valley Sober House were accosted by street dealers each day. Some residents cycled back and forth from Evergreen to the sober houses, as long as the insurers kept paying. The irony that Dr. Singer had provided the medications that landed patients in his rehabs never concerned him.

By 2010, Dr. Singer's little business in rehabilitation was thriving. His income from the Evergreen facility and the two sober houses exceeded a million dollars annually. Most of his income was in the form of insurance checks from both government and private insurers. His fine administrator, Delores, became extremely sophisticated with probing the bureaucratic intricacies of getting payment. Each month, his resident checks came in like clockwork.

But that was not enough for Dr. Singer. He often witnessed empty beds at his facilities, which disturbed him. Despite the doctor's misgivings about his partner, he again reached out to Doctor C in this new venture. Dr. Singer needed more new patients, and Doctor C had such people on the street. They were known as "body brokers."

Chapter 16: Spring Valley Sober House

KELSEY ENTERED THE SPRING VALLEY Sober House in June of 2010. She regretted the termination of her individual and group counseling at Evergreen, but she felt surprisingly confident that she would not relapse. Therapy had provided her with insight about her behavior, specifically what the drugs replaced that she needed to confront. Her awareness that she had a pretty shitty upbringing, but still was a good person worthy of love, resonated within her. The brief euphoria of any drug did not match the rewards that a sober life offered. Her counselors had helped clarify her passion for art, as well as the idea that she was someone who deserved to be loved. She now had specific goals to be an artist, and have a family one day with whom she could give unconditional love.

Kelsey had to admit, the all-girl Spring Valley was a step down from Evergreen. The tired, ranch-style home housed a total of nine women. It sat in a neighborhood of similarly styled Springvale homes, many of which were as neglected as the Sober House. The area consisted of some vacant commercial properties, a "dollar" store, a McDonald's, and several liquor stores. Upon entering the house, Kelsey was greeted by a cigarette smell that seemed to be a living organism buried within the walls of chipped gray paint. The ancient Salvation Army furniture looked like it might collapse at any moment. Kelsey observed a simple shotgun front-to-back layout of the small home - living room on the left, dining room on the right, a large communal kitchen, followed by two bedrooms on each side in the rear. Kelsey would occupy a bedroom on the left with two other residents. The other two bedrooms on the right were occupied by six more women. The last bedroom adjacent to Kelsey's was occupied by Spring Valley's director, Lucinda Olivera.

Lucinda Olivera greeted Kelsey upon her arrival. A tall, regal-appearing Hispanic woman in her forties, Lucinda had short hair,

The Girl Who Woke Up in the Morgue

gold earrings that almost hit her broad shoulders, and a pleasant smile. Kelsey soon saw that pleasant smile turn into the stern look of a drill instructor as she laid out the rules of the house. Random urine samples were taken at her staff's discretion, and any positive test meant ouster from the house. Residents were assigned chores each week and were expected to help prepare meals. The women were allowed to leave the home each day from 9 to 5 only to work, attend drug meetings, or go to school. Evenings were devoted to group meetings, which were started promptly at 7:00 PM. A nervous Kelsey's told Lucinda she understood the rules, quickly realizing why Lucinda was known to all in the home as "Big Lou."

Kelsey was assigned the top bunk in her small bedroom. The lower bunk was occupied by Fran, a tiny, raven-haired woman in her thirties with sad brown eyes. Janice, a young woman a bit older than Kelsey, occupied her own single bed in the tight quarters. Kelsey was surprised to learn that Fran and Janice were very familiar with Spring Valley. Fran said in a tired voice, "We are three-timers, but some have been in and out even more."

Unlike the quiet Fran, who kept mostly to herself, the saucy, gum-chewing Janice projected a chip-on-her-shoulder street smart persona. She had ivory white skin layered with freckles and bright red hair. The Squeaky Fromme lookalike quickly took Kelsey under her wing. Each day, they left the home promptly at 9:00 a.m., purportedly to go to a drug meeting. Instead, they often met Janice's boyfriend Bruce, who was a resident of Spring Valley's Sober House for male addicts. Kelsey learned that Janice and Bruce had been a couple for two years, and she admired the way Janice stood by Bruce, who showed more scars from his addiction. His limp body seemed devoid of muscle, and his head seemed to always hang below his shoulders. But it was his eyes that struck Kelsey. They were tired eyes, devoid of any sparkle. He had the type of hang-dog, hopeless look that seemed to convey that life had given up on him, or vice versa.

Kelsey was surprised to see that despite "Big Lou's" admonitions, the Sober House had rules but few followed them. At night, their group meetings might be attended by as few as two to four residents. Others might be sleeping, and some even often returned to the home after curfew. Faces changed frequently in the house – Kelsey returned one day to see that Fran had moved out. In a couple of days, a young girl, Amy, about the age of Kelsey, occupied the top bunk. She appeared glassy-eyed to Kelsey, and her nausea convinced Kelsey that she was actively using. She shared her suspicions with Janice, who said, "No shit!" between snaps of bubble gum.

Despite the limitations in size, Kelsey was the first person at group meetings. Often it might be Kelsey and one or two others. Strictly peer-based, residents at the meetings shared their hellish journeys of drug addiction. Kelsey absorbed the common narratives that all of them shared - a powerful sense of shame that they had let down those who loved them; their regret that sobriety – whether for one week or one year - was one weak moment away from relapse; and that they all hated that the pursuit of drugs was the main goal of their lives when using.

In return, Kelsey experienced the genuine support that all these addicts gave her when she shared her own experiences. The older addicts encouraged the youthful Kelsey to pursue her passion for art. Experiencing the warmth from those damaged souls, Kelsey tearfully realized it was as if the older residents were talking to their younger selves. Kelsey promised herself that would not be her.

Kelsey and Janice continued their long walks with one another each morning. They were always careful to avoid the people wheeling carts of redeemable bottles, or shady street people gathering early on corners near the Sober House. They talked, and one day as Kelsey was sharing her appreciation for the previous night's group meeting, in her own inimitable style, Janice interrupted her and blurted out, "Spring Valley is a fucking joke!" Stunned, Kelsey asked what she meant. "It's all about the fucking money," Janice said, and went on to explain that residents moved in and out of the home depending on who paid Spring Valley. "Some of the residents are considered disabled, and Medicare will pay for treatments. Others like you have private insurance, and their companies will pay for treatment." Janice then said, "These places hit the jackpot when there is a relapse – they are paid again for treatment at places like Evergreen. I've done this double run twice."

Incredulous, Kelsey said, "So these places want you to relapse, so they can get more money?" Janice responded, "Don't be fucking stupid, Kelsey. You see people high in the house. Where do you think they are getting the drugs?" She reached into her pocket and pulled out a bunch of signed prescriptions. "Where did you get that?" a shocked Kelsey demanded. "You don't want to know the answer. But everyone in the house knows I can get pills. I gave some Zanax to Amy before her discharge.

The Girl Who Woke Up in the Morgue

Kelsey could not believe what she was hearing. She wanted to get out of the Sober House as quickly as possible. She had worked too hard on her sobriety to be tempted in this intimate setting. She placed a call to her uncle, George Fulton, and asked if she could return to her job and apartment. After a brief hesitation, George said that he could not allow Kelsey to work at the company any longer. He said the sensitive nature of her work and the risk of bad publicity for the company precluded her employment there. He quickly added that she could stay in the apartment as long as she needed to, or until she got another job. He even suggested that Kelsey might want to return to her mother. Little did he know, thought Kelsey, that she had not talked to her angry mother in two months. Kelsey said, "Does my grandmother know about this?" "Yes," George said. Kelsey thought this explained why Grace had not reached out to her for some time.

Kelsey went to her room dispirited and crying after the call to her uncle. She realized her initial instincts about the Fultons were correct. She beat herself up for fantasizing that they truly cared for her. Kelsey sat on her bed pondering her future, concerned that any instability could cause her to relapse. Her concerns were interrupted by the loud voice of

Big Lou: "Kelsey, you got a visitor." Drying her eyes, Kelsey walked to the living room. Sitting in a tiny, brittle rocking chair was the smiling face of Sonny Fiorentino. "There's my friend Kelsey. How are you doing?" he said. Kelsey admitted, "I've had better days." She looked down, concerned that Sonny would see her red eyes. Sonny laughed, "I've been hearing great things about your recovery. I'm not surprised. You know you and I have a special connection with one another, right?" said an upbeat Sonny.

Kelsey tried to laugh, but only tears came from her heaving body. In almost one breath, a surprised Kelsey blurted to Sonny about why she wanted to leave the house, how the Fultons had fired her from her job, and how scared and she was about her future. Sonny just listened, seeming to move closer to her with each breath. When Kelsey was done with her long confession, Sonny was close enough to hug her.

Sonny then gripped Kelsey by both shoulders and looked deeply into her eyes. "Since the first time I saw you, I knew you were a special young lady. Unfortunately, because we thought you'd passed away, I didn't think I would find out how special you were. But you've got a second chance, Kelsey--something the young people I'm now burying did not get. So, you see, we are a special team, right?" For the first time, Kelsey smiled and said, "I guess you're right." Sonny continued, "You see, Kelsey, I have spent my whole life taking care of my family and my business. In the process, I forgot to take care of myself. My passion right now is to help all the young people in Springdale who are abusing drugs." He laughed ruefully, "My new mission as a funeral director is not to bury any more young people – just old ones like me."

Kelsey was a bit perplexed as Sonny rambled on and on about the dangers in the community. Sonny droned on, "Is this my only function in life, to bury the dead? I realize now that my job is to help the living." As he spoke, Kelsey thought to herself that he seemed to be having a mid-life crisis. Sonny surprised Kelsey with the intensity of his next remarks. "The first young person I want to help is you. How about you come to work for me?" Kelsey laughed, "You want me to be a funeral director?" "Maybe," Sonny answered, "I have lots of people who work for me in a variety of roles, and I do have two female funeral directors. You can assist people who might need your smiling eyes.

"I have a huge apartment in my funeral home with five bedrooms, and you can live there as long as you want. It is so big, we might not see each other for days." Kelsey could barely process what Sonny was offering her. Unlike her initial instincts with the Fultons, Kelsey knew in her bones that Sonny was sincere. She shook her head affirmatively.

"Two conditions," said Sonny, "You have to continue addiction counseling and go to school for whatever you want to study. I'll pay for it." Kelsey could not believe her ears. "I want to take art classes," she said. "Art, huh?" said Sonny, "I might need an artist at the funeral home someday." Kelsey nervously asked Sonny when she could move in, almost fearing that Sonny would change his mind. "You can come when you leave the Spring Valley Sober House," said Sonny. "I'm leaving right now," said Kelsey, running to grab all her belongings in her suitcase. Sonny smiled and said, "Great."

Chapter 17:
Kelsey, The Art Student

IT WAS JANUARY 2012, and Kelsey had been sober and living at Sonny's Funeral Home for a year. Now almost twenty, Kelsey's physical appearance had matured. No more nose ring. Her slight overbite, over which she was so self-conscious, had been corrected by braces, provided by Sonny. Her hairdresser had framed her face in a modern shag style that gave body to her lean face. Her dark face and features gave her an exotic look that drew the attention of her fellow art students

With Sonny's encouragement, Kelsey was an art student at the Springdale Art Institute. She eagerly absorbed the concepts in art theory three days per week. Intellectually stimulated, she also pursued the biographies of great artists on her own. She was particularly drawn to the great portrait artists, such as Rembrandt and DaVinci.

Kelsey also continued her individual psychological therapy with the encouragement of Sonny. Kelsey's therapy continued to probe the forces that led her to addiction. Kelsey confronted the abandonment issues by her dad, as well as her mom's hysteric personality. Kelsey had to admit that, with her therapist's help, she was a person worthy of love. Kelsey was learning to love herself in this supportive environment.

That environment was also a happier one for Sonny. He loved having company in his expansive home. Kelsey's art now populated the living and dining rooms, giving color and life to his home. Beyond the art, Sonny looked at Kelsey like a proud father who sees his adolescent daughter maturing before his eyes. She was a natural star in the funeral business, offering genuine compassion to the bereaved. Sonny had Kelsey by his side when he made funeral arrangements. He thought Kelsey possessed the most important ingredient that a good funeral director requires – a good heart. "Who knows?" Sonny said to himself more than once, "maybe Kelsey will go to mortuary school one day."

Kelsey's relationship with her mom had also been tentatively renewed. It was renewed

The Girl Who Woke Up in the Morgue

in a strange way – with the unexpected death of her grandmother, Grace Fulton, three months earlier. George and Frank Fulton arrived in Sonny's funeral home to report Grace's death the night before. They were surprised, actually shocked, to see their niece Kelsey sitting with Sonny. It lent a strange twist to the conference, because it now involved Grace's granddaughter. Kelsey, feeling guilty that she had not reached out to Grace recently, asked her uncles what happened. George responded that their eighty-five-year-old mother must have had a silent heart attack during the night. George said through tears, "She went to bed healthy and simply did not wake up." Frank added, "I had talked to her at 8 p.m. and she sounded fine." An upset Kelsey asked Sonny if she could leave the conference. She retreated to her room and immediately took out art tools. She would draw a portrait of Grace, no matter how poorly it came out. She wanted to acknowledge the woman who'd tried to make her a part of the Fulton family. Even if her grandmother's efforts were not successful, thought Kelsey, it had brought her to Springdale.

Sonny proceeded to make funeral arrangements with George and Frank Fulton. Sonny told the men they would have his largest chapel, given the prominence of the family. Sonny almost fell off his chair at the Fultons response. Frank said, "We are not having any services for our mom. These were her wishes, Sonny." They wanted no viewing and a direct cremation of their mom. They also told Sonny not to even post her death on his website. Perhaps looking at Sonny's face, which registered a countenance that the community would not have a chance to say goodbye to the prominent woman, Frank said, "We will say our own goodbyes privately as a family, Sonny."

Following their departure, Sonny slowly went up to Kelsey's bedroom. He knocked on the door and asked if he could enter. He proceeded to tell Kelsey what the family wanted for Grace's funeral arrangements. The stunned Kelsey sobbed on Sonny's shoulder, "She was the only Fulton who cared about me." Aware of Kelsey's relationship with her mom, Sonny gently said, "Isn't there another Fulton who cares for you?" A thoughtful Kelsey agreed, "I'm calling my mom."

Despite what the Fultons preferred, Sonny had Grace Fulton dressed in an evening gown and had her gray hair smartly styled.

On the day of Grace's cremation, Sonny led Kelsey and her mom Susan down to the morgue, where Grace lay in a simple wood

The Girl Who Woke Up in the Morgue

casket. It was the same morgue where Kelsey had lain almost two years earlier. Susan bowed to the casket, caressed her mom's face, and asked for forgiveness. "I was a terrible daughter, Mom. I'm so sorry that I never told you I love you." Kelsey instinctively went to her mother's side and said, "She hears you now, Mom. Talk to her." And that was what Susan did for the next fifteen minutes. Through tears and laughter, Susan revealed how difficult she was as a child and teenager. Throughout her bitter estrangement with the family, Susan confirmed that her mom had always reached out to her. Kelsey said goodbye to her grandmother as the casket was loaded into the hearse for the journey to the crematory. Mother and daughter collapsed in each other's arms as the hearse drove away.

Something changed in Susan with her mom's death. Perhaps it was the awareness that life was fragile, and she had a chance to correct her mistakes. She had a chance to tell her daughter Kelsey what her own feelings were, face-to-face. For the first time in years, Susan told Kelsey, "I love you." She then turned to Sonny, gave him a big hug, and thanked him for taking care of her daughter.

As he was embraced, Sonny smiled to himself as he thought about how things had changed. When Sonny had first met Susan the previous day, he was met with suspicion. In her inimitable style Susan demanded, "Why the fuck is my daughter living in a funeral home?" Sonny also grasped her deeper meaning. It was Kelsey who intervened. "Sonny is the kindest man I've ever known, Mom. I wish my dad was like him." A more relaxed Susan seemed to understand the relationship between her daughter and Sonny. Susan grasped that Kelsey was maturing in a good way through Sonny's influence.

Her mother stayed the night in the funeral home. "I can't believe I'm sleeping in a funeral home," she repeated over and over. They had a fun night in the apartment above the sad chapels below. Kelsey cooked her mom dinner, a habit she had started for Sonny, who previously had often dined on takeout or pizza. Susan admired her daughter's artwork displayed on easels that Sonny had set up. The next day, mother and daughter said, "I love you," as Susan left to return home.

Three days later, Sonny and Kelsey sat with another family who were burying a child. This was a young woman, aged twenty-two. The coroner told them she'd died of an opiate overdose. As the young lady's dad spoke, Sonny thought the man looked vaguely familiar. It then dawned on him: the dad was the man from the Carson boy's funeral who had commented that drugs would never touch his family. Sonny wished he had been wrong when he'd told the man that drugs could cross anyone's path.

The family had waged a year-long battle to get their daughter off oxycodone. A gymnast, the daughter had been given opioids at the age of nineteen for a tear in one of her hamstrings. With no warning from the doctors of a possible addiction, the parents were unaware what was occurring. For a year, their wonderful and popular daughter hid her growing addiction. The parents learned of it when their daughter forged checks on their account. Their daughter's life spiraled out of control as she went in and out of treatment. When she stole money from her grandmother at her grandfather's funeral, the family had had enough. Six months earlier, they had kicked her out of the house.

What they learned in retrospect was that their daughter's opiate addiction proved too costly for her. They told Sonny that Oxycodone or Dilaudid pills often sold for $50 a pill. Heroin was a cheaper drug with a more intense high. Some sold for as little as $10 a bag, and there was a plentiful supply of it in Springdale.. Snorting the drug quickly turned into shooting heroin for a quicker, more powerful result.

Stephen Rocco

Sonny listened as the tearful parents regretted their "tough love" approach. They told Sonny that their guilty daughter had told them she would never put a needle in her arm. She was a champion gymnast, an athlete who would not even take an aspirin for a headache. Sonny listened silently, fuming at this scourge, offering the only encouragement he could. He had seen many good families, just like theirs, suffer something that had no reflection on them as parents.

For Kelsey, sitting with Sonny as usual, these sad conferences only reinforced her own sobriety. She realized how quickly she'd descended to near death.

Two days later, Sonny's funeral home was filled to capacity with people attendeding the funeral of the young girl. Coaches, teachers, and friends stood in long lines to console her family. Sonny could not escape the words of these visitors: "she was such a good girl." "She had so much potential." "What a shame."

Sonny spent a restless night thinking about what he now viewed as a pandemic. He thought to himself, "We can't let this go on." He decided to call Skip in the morning to have one of their coffee updates. They must get someone to investigate these cases. They must become more aggressive.

The Girl Who Woke Up in the Morgue

For Kelsey, lying in bed in the adjoining room, this funeral was equally upsetting. But she was upset for a different reason. She had seen Taylor at the funeral. She had not seen or talked to him since her hospitalization. They engaged in some small talk, but she could not get over how much he had changed. His denim slacks had been replaced by stylish black leather slacks and a matching jacket. He moved with a confident swagger, accompanied by a friend. His friend was the scary individual Kelsey had met twice before: Doctor C!

Chapter 18: The Undercover Investigation

SONNY FIORENTINO AND SKIP LEBLANC had one of their bi-weekly meetings about their opiate concerns. They were joined by a new face, however. Felix Osborn was a private investigator who had recently contacted Sonny. Felix had been hired by the Fischer family. Sonny had buried their son, who had died from an overdose, a month earlier. His dad, Bob Fischer, now had a new mission in life. That was to honor his son by finding out how and why these drugs were in the Springdale community. His efforts would not bring his son back, thought Mr. Fischer, but they could prevent more deaths.

Felix Osborn might be someone you would overlook on first sight. Short, no taller than 5'4", but in good shape and with a bit of remaining fuzz on the sides of his bald palate, Felix's eyes were hidden behind thick glasses. Those glasses, however, hid eyes with a burning intensity. As a youth on the playgrounds, classmates learned not to taunt him with "Felix" jokes. Felix had no problem sticking up for himself. Just as importantly, he enjoyed going at it with bullies who bothered his weaker classmates.

Felix, now forty, had recently retired after a twenty-year career with the Navy. He was an intelligence officer whose official duty was to monitor and analyze activities that posed a risk to national security. This job fit Felix perfectly. It combined his keen intelligence with his determined tenacity. The broad description had taken him around the world: to Columbia to analyze the transfer patterns of the drug cartel, to Iraq and the assimilation of data to save American lives in battle. Acquiring vital information to help America consumed the detail-oriented Felix. This probably explained why Felix had never married. His "marriage" to the Navy and his constant travel precluded that.

Felix retired as a lieutenant in the U.S. Navy in 2009, receiving numerous citations for leadership. He was ready for the next phase of his life, determined to put his feet down in one place. He chose Springdale because his beloved only sibling, Nancy, lived there. Nancy was a recent divorcee, so Felix felt like a surrogate father to his niece Susan and nephew Sam.

Felix opened his cybersecurity business shortly after moving to Springdale. Business picked up quickly, mostly from businesses such as banks and retailers who needed online protection. Felix built a quick reputation, not only in building cyber-safeguards, but in identifying and solving breaches in his clients' security systems.

So it was a bit of a surprise that Felix had offered his technical services to the men. Skip thought to himself, how is a cyber-expert going to help this investigation? Felix put Skip's concerns to bed quickly. He told Sonny that he knew the kids were using drugs in the funeral home bathroom the night of the Fischer wake. Sonny was surprised, since not many people were aware of this. Felix explained that he had taken his niece to the wake that night, since she was a classmate of a younger Fischer child. While in the restroom, Felix saw a young man with a bag full of pills that he was handing out to his friends.

Felix had instinctively acted and took the pills from the young man. He demanded to know from the youth where he got the pills.

The Girl Who Woke Up in the Morgue

The young man ran out of the bathroom with his friends, but not before muttering, "They are everywhere – got them in Greenville."

Felix then reached into his pocket and gave the plastic bag to Detective LeBlanc. "They are 50 mg. hydrocodone pills," said Felix, "enough to kill a horse, said a pharmacist I know." Felix was not done with his surprises. He reached back into his pocket and produced a prescription bottle. It contained sixty oxycodone pills, each 30 mg. He showed the bottle to the other men. Skip noticed that the pills were prescribed by the nearby Greenville Wellness and Pain Clinic. They were filled by a Greenville pharmacy adjacent to the clinic.

Felix then told the stunned men that he had gone to the pain clinic complaining of a bad back. After barely ten minutes with a Dr. Miller, he was prescribed the sixty pills. His back was not tested in any way other than a cursory tracing of the contour of his back. Dr. Miller diagnosed a bulging disc and told him to return in a month if the pills did not work. The doctor even suggested that Felix get the pills from the pharmacy across the street. "They take all kinds of insurance," said Dr. Miller, who was himself only too happy to bill his $600 "exam" fee to Felix's military insurance.

Skip LeBlanc could not believe the story. "You're telling me this Dr. Miller did not schedule any MRI of your back?" "That's correct," replied Felix, "and I was not alone. The waiting room was filled with people of all ages."

Felix was not done with surprises. While at the Greenville clinic, he struck up a conversation with a long-haul truck driver. The driver told him that he could not survive his job without these oxys. Felix questioned the safety issues driving on medication, which the man poo-pooed. "I've been on them so long, I don't get a buzz. I'm mostly concerned I'll run out of pills on the road." The driver went on to explain to Felix that was why he bounced from the Greenville clinic to the one in Springdale. He encouraged Felix to go to the Springdale Family Clinic if he needed pills before the thirty-day period. "They give out prescriptions like candy," said the truck driver with a wink.

By now the slack-jawed Skip and Sonny were beyond amazed by these revelations. Felix continued, "So I went to the Springdale Family and Pain Clinic, run by this Dr. Jerome Singer. I just sat in the waiting room and watched the bevy of patients going in and out of the offices. In one hour, I saw thirty patients go from check-in to departure. I also observed that many of these patients often came in with someone. It looked suspicious to me as, once inside, they did not talk or even look at each other. I followed one of these pairs out of the door. I then saw one party handing something to the other."

An angry Sonny asked, "Is it possible that doctors, pharmacists, and dealers are working together to poison Springdale? How could our doctors, who are supposed to save people, shit on their oaths?"

Skip immediately captured the possible significance of the exchange. "They might be recruiting people on the streets to become patients. They would then pay that person for the prescription, or if needed, accompany him to the pharmacy." It seemed to dawn on the three gentlemen that this conspiracy may go deeper than they had ever imagined.

Sonny could not believe that Dr. Singer, the man he had known as a child and whose dad was beloved in Springdale, could succumb to this type of greed.

Felix was not surprised at all, given his secretive work for the government. He told them this sort of liaison had been common in the drug wars of Columbia, and could be taking place here in Springdale. "When it comes to greed, people can justify any of their actions, even murder."

Detective LeBlanc spoke up and thanked Felix for his work. He shared with Sonny and Felix that one good thing was that Chief Powell had retired. The new chief was open to more resources devoted to an opioid investigation. Skip could have his detectives develop some informants, "but that will take time." Sonny slammed the table. "We don't have time – I don't want to bury any more young people!"

He even startled himself in his anger, to the point that no one noticed a new person in the room. Kelsey had been present for a bit and wanted to be a part of the discussion. "I can help," Kelsey said calmly. Felix, who had never met Kelsey, was immediately impressed by this young woman's physical stature, but also her quiet confidence.

After Kelsey was introduced to Felix, she told the men she could go undercover, given her experiences. She knew some people who had connections to the scene, such as her old boyfriend Taylor. A protective Sonny immediately responded, "No! It is not safe" Non-plussed, Kelsey turned to Detective LeBlanc. "How long might it take for your detective to go undercover and get information?" Skip admitted that it could take at least six months, if not longer. Kelsey turned to Sonny. "We don't have the time. Six months

The Girl Who Woke Up in the Morgue

may mean thousands more pills in Springdale."

Detective LeBlanc thought Kelsey's plan might make sense. "If I get more evidence, Sonny, I can call in the DEA. If the court allows Kelsey to wear a wire, it's our best shot to stop this scourge. I'll make sure my men keep a close eye on Kelsey."

Felix was impressed by Kelsey's offer to help the investigation. She reminded him why he went into government service – a selfless need to help others. He thought to himself that she would make a great soldier. "Wearing a wire is not like in the old days," said Felix. "I can put an audio recorder that will pick up sound from a hundred feet away into a ring. I can put a two-way camera on your bracelet, Kelsey, where police see the same images as you do instantaneously." "Wow!" said Skip. "I didn't even know technology had advanced that quickly." A reluctant Sonny seemed to soften with Felix's information. "So, she will never be out of your sight, Skip?" "Correct."

The meeting at the funeral home soon ended. Skip said, "I'll go to Chief Stratton tomorrow and start the process for Kelsey to be a confidential informant. We have to get the District Attorney on board before they petition the Court for a wire. I'll give them all the evidence we have. Additionally, I'll have my investigators continue to monitor the traffic at Dr. Singer's practices in Springdale and Greenville.

Two days later, Sonny got the bad news. As Kelsey listened in on the phone call, she heard Skip say that the district attorney would not act. They needed more evidence. An exasperated Sonny yelled into the phone, "Do they want me to bury more bodies?" He listened as Skip told him to be patient. "My men are getting more information each day. I think in a couple of weeks, we can convince the district attorney." A disappointed Sonny said, "Thanks, Skip. Sorry, I know you want to help."

Kelsey silently told herself that they could not waste any more time. She had a plan. She picked up the phone and called her new friend Felix.

Chapter 19: Reunion with Taylor

THE NEXT DAY, KELSEY fingered her new key chain as she nervously called her old boyfriend Taylor. "Sure," Taylor responded readily when Kelsey asked if they could go to lunch. "How about tomorrow, around 1 p.m.?" Taylor then received the surprise of his life when he asked Kelsey where he should pick her up. "What, you live in the funeral home that you almost died in?" Taylor repeated this over and over.

It seemed to trigger a new guilt in Taylor. "You know, Kel, I'm sorry I left you that night." Kelsey cut him off, "Stop it. No one put the drugs in my mouth. We can talk about this tomorrow over lunch." "Sure," said Taylor. "See you at the funeral home at 1 p.m.

Stephen Rocco

As Kelsey put down the phone, she thought that Taylor sounded great. I hope he's sober, she thought. While no longer in "love" with Taylor, she genuinely liked him. They had bonded over art. He was her first true love. But those feelings could not preclude what she was about to do.

Her call to Felix the previous day was to inquire if he would help her record her conversation with Taylor. Felix arrived the next day with a small key chain she could keep in her purse. The key chain would record the conversation. Kelsey then revealed her plan to Felix. "I know our conversation can't be used in court, but Taylor knows a lot about the organization. He knows how the pills are getting to the street."

Felix gave the key chain to Kelsey on one condition. He would follow Taylor's car on his own, to make sure she was safe. "It's just a lunch, you worrywart," chuckled Kelsey. But Felix remained steadfast, and Kelsey finally agreed to his condition.

The next morning, Felix showed up and promptly delivered a plan with military precision. "Don't ask Taylor too many questions at first. Let him get comfortable. Make good eye contact." Interrupting Felix, Kelsey said, "You worry too much. It's just a meeting with a guy I used to date. I think I can handle that." Felix was adamant. "I know, Kelsey, but with the kind of money involved, these guys mean business. Just be careful, OK? I won't let you out of my sight."

At about 1 o'clock, Taylor pulled up in a new Jeep Wrangler. "Wow, I can't believe you live in a funeral home, Kel," said a smiling Taylor. "Doesn't it creep you out?" Kelsey smiled back, "No, it's actually comforting to live here. I see it as a house that heals people." "Not me," said Taylor. "I couldn't do it."

Kelsey was impressed a bit by the changes in her friend. Taylor no longer wore everyday clothes so casual that one outfit looked like another – jeans and sweatshirts. No, he had an expensive black leather coat and tight designer jeans. His hands no longer bore rings on every finger. Most importantly, Taylor said that he had been off opiates for six months. As they drove to lunch, Taylor made an offhanded comment: "I'm making too much money to use that shit." Kelsey noticed that Felix was following closely behind them.

Over a leisurely lunch, observed by Felix, the two friends caught up with each other's lives. Kelsey had brought some of her art work from her classes. Taylor was impressed. Kelsey encouraged him to take a class with her. "Don't have time," said Taylor. This led to a long discussion about Taylor's life since

Kelsey's overdose. "You know I feel terrible about that night," began a misty-eyed Taylor. "I know," said Kelsey, "but it was the best thing that happened to me, Taylor. It got me sober." Taylor agreed. "That was a wakeup moment for me, Kelsey. I stopped using right after that." The more and more intimate conversation then moved to Taylor's life today.

What Taylor slowly revealed to Kelsey was that while he did not use drugs, he was in the opiate business. Careful not to say whom he worked for, Taylor said he was perfectly placed in his new business. He had street contacts to distribute pills and suppliers who could get him as many pills as he needed. Kelsey thought to herself, this explains how he afforded that Jeep. She briefly opened her purse, satisfied that the key chain was working.

Careful not to show her disgust, Kelsey feigned that she was enthralled with Taylor's business acumen. "It looks like you will make a lot of money in this business," she forced herself to say. "Yes, the sky's the limit," said a contented Taylor as the couple enjoyed sitting at the outdoor café.

A calculating Kelsey began to explain that while she enjoyed her life at the funeral home, it did not pay her bills. She told Taylor that without more income, she would have to drop out of art school.

Taylor nodded in sympathy. Then, thoughtful for a few moments, he said, "Maybe I can help." He went on to reveal that his partners were often looking for new recruiters. "What's a recruiter?" asked Kelsey. Taylor explained that in the opiate business, you constantly needed new customers. A new supply of people to get prescriptions ensured more profits. "How do you get these patients?" asked a stunned Kelsey. "Not today," answered Taylor. "Let me talk to my bosses about you, and we will see where it goes." Then Taylor looked up, raised his hand and said, "Another cappuccino, please."

After lunch, Kelsey arrived back at the funeral home to find a nervous Felix waiting for her. "This might go deeper than we even imagined, Kelsey. After listening to Taylor's words, I don't want you to meet him again. Let's wait until Skip gets more information before meeting them." Kelsey began to object, but Felix was adamant that she not meet Taylor's bosses. "Promise me you will not meet again with Taylor." Recognizing the intensity in Felix's eyes, Kelsey agreed, "I'll wait."

After Felix left, Kelsey went back to her large bedroom in the funeral home. She sadly looked out the window at the town of Springdale below and wondered if this beautiful town was cursed. As she gazed out the window, she ruminated on her lunch with Taylor. "How many people are involved in this conspiracy?" Kelsey could not believe that this word had come naturally to her mind: "conspiracy." How could it be otherwise, Kelsey asked herself?

That night, Kelsey prepared a special dinner for Sonny. Since he was a boy, he'd had a penchant for fish but coveted one that few other people, even Italians, cared for: anchovies. Sonny's friends even made faces when he ordered anchovy pizza. That never bothered him; just more slices for him.

One of the benefits of having Kelsey live with him was that he no longer ate meals alone. No more sterile anchovy pizzas delivered from Nana's to his mansion on the hill. One night, Sonny shared with Kelsey that as a boy, his mother would make him a special meal – spaghetti aioli with anchovies. It was a traditional Italian meal that few restaurants served, since it was not popular.

Kelsey wanted to do something nice for the man who was more of a father to her than anyone. She had found a recipe online and crossed her fingers that it was even edible. She was relieved to see Sonny smiling after his first bite. She was even happier when Sonny asked for a second helping.

It was in this convivial atmosphere that Kelsey shared her meeting with Taylor. She shared her thoughts with Sonny about the network of people involved in this scheme. She mentioned the word "conspiracy" to Sonny. Sonny somberly pondered the significance of Kelsey's suspicions. He thought of all the young faces he'd buried who were victims of greed. A conspiracy implied to Sonny layers of people, all guided by a desire to poison his beloved community.

Kelsey then revealed that she was going to speak to Taylor again. "No!" shouted Sonny. "This is not safe. Let Skip's men get the evidence." Kelsey had never seen Sonny so angry. "With this much money involved, no one is safe. Please, Kelsey, promise me you will not meet Taylor again." "I promise," said Kelsey, relieved that she had not told Sonny about the secret recording.

Sonny's reaction alerted Kelsey to the dangerous world she was entering. It also told her that she had to be careful not to tell anyone else about her new plan – not even Felix. She awaited Taylor's call.

Chapter 20:
Kelsey's Meeting with Dr. Singer

A NERVOUS KELSEY did not hear from Taylor for one week. When she did, he asked if she was available to meet on Sunday. "Sure," said Kelsey, "Where are we going?" "I'll tell you Sunday." With Felix's military suggestion in mind, Kelsey said, "Okay." She did not want to raise any suspicions by probing the issue any further.

On the appointed day, a brilliant, sunny day, she had Taylor pick her up in downtown Springdale. She did not want a nervous Sonny following her. A reserved Taylor gave Kelsey a quick peck on the cheek as she entered the jeep. "If it's okay, my bosses want to meet you on their boat." "Sure," said a tense Kelsey, fingering her key chain, telling herself to stay cool.

The couple was soon at the gates of Springdale Yacht Club. Although they engaged in conversation, Kelsey sensed that Taylor was not himself. He seemed distracted and avoided her gaze. Kelsey felt a growing surge of tension in her gut, which she tried to repress. She reached into her purse and glanced at the audio recorder.

Soon they were before the largest boat in the marina, named "Seaduction." Taylor was wrong. The "Seaduction" was not a boat, but a yacht. It was a three-level, towering sixty-foot palace that had open and closed decks, with custom teak furniture. In a later, private tour by her hosts, Kelsey admired a galley that put Sonny's kitchen to shame. Below this deck were three sleeping cabins and two full heads with showers.

Kelsey's admiration was quickly ended by the four hands that helped her aboard. Two of those belonged to the imposing fellow she had seen at the party she'd attended with Taylor, and at her hospital bed. Taylor quickly introduced Kelsey to him. "You remember Doctor C, Kel?" How could she forget? His black leather coat had been replaced by a beach hoodie and a tight bathing suit that went up high on his thighs. But his eyes were as dark as Kelsey remembered them. "Watch your step," he said to Kelsey in a cold, business-like manner. Kelsey observed that Doctor C's smile was so tight, you could not see his teeth. "Sure," said Kelsey. "How have you been?"

On the other side of Kelsey, helping her onto the boat, was another middle-aged man with an easier smile. "Kel, this is Dr. Jerome Singer. This is his boat." "Oh, hello," smiled Kelsey. "I've heard Sonny talk about you." Dr. Singer looked puzzled. "Sonny?" Taylor responded, "That's the funeral director I told you about, who saved Kelsey. She lives with him." "Ah, that's right," said Dr. Singer. "How could I forget that? Sonny is a great guy. He was always a great friend of my dad. That's quite a thing that happened to you, Kelsey." Before she could respond, Doctor C piped in, "How did it feel to wake up in the morgue?" Kelsey could simply offer, "Lucky," to which a smiling Dr. Singer agreed, "Good answer." Dr. Singer surprised Kelsey when he then asked her how she was related to the Fulton family. He commented that he was a good friend of her family and had some mutual business interests.

Kelsey was next given a quick tour of the impressive yacht, and met the other guests. Beyond Taylor and the two men, the captain and two young women not much older than Kelsey were aboard. The young ladies were wearing two-piece bikinis that were so revealing that little flesh was covered. The women were asked to make drinks for the group, and Kelsey watched as the two men's eyes drifted to the "Brazilian" style bottoms of their scanty bikinis as they walked toward the bar. Doctor C looked at Kelsey and smirked, "Nothing stronger than a ginger ale for you?"

Kelsey anxiously waited for the types of questions that she had prepared for. They never came. Dr. Singer was content to tell Kelsey about their itinerary. They would cruise for a few hours, and then the girls would prepare lunch. Doctor C did not say much, but his body language suggested that he was somehow sizing Kelsey up.

Dr. Singer seemed genuinely interested in Kelsey's art career. "Maybe you can do a portrait of me someday?" Taylor, too, was supportive of her talents. "She is really talented. I wish I could draw like her." Kelsey smiled, "You have talents of your own." Doctor C looked at Taylor and responded sarcastically, "You can draw?" An embarrassed Taylor, obviously kowtowing to Doctor C answered, "I guess I don't have time to draw these days." Kelsey noticed this dynamic between Taylor and Doctor C, and felt bad for Taylor. She said to herself, "What does this guy have on Taylor?"

Oblivious to this dynamic playing out, Dr. Singer told Kelsey about his own career. He saw his dad choose a medical career, but never reap its benefits. "I vowed that when I became a doctor, I would work as hard as my dad, but reap the financial benefits." Looking around, he proudly said, "This is what I work for, Kelsey."

At some point Taylor went up to the sun pad in the bow of the boat where the young ladies were tanning. Alone with the men, Kelsey took a deep breath, and decided to ask a question. She made sure her purse with the activated recorder was close to her side. "Taylor told me that you might have some work for me. I have tuition coming, and ..." Dr. Singer interrupted her and put his fingers to his lips. "Shh, we just wanted to meet you today Kelsey. We can discuss that matter later." He then encouraged Kelsey to join the ladies on the bow. As she left to do just that, Kelsey observed the doctor and Doctor C pull their chairs close together in discussion.

Kelsey sat with the two young ladies with the taut bodies. One said, "I hope you brought a bathing suit." Taylor apologized, "Sorry, Kel. I should have told you we were going on the boat." She was actually relieved, as her body

The Girl Who Woke Up in the Morgue

did not match the taut ones on board. "That's okay, Taylor." As the young people sat there enjoying the sun, the captain on the fly bridge shouted down to Taylor, "The bosses want to see you." Taylor quickly went to the stern of the boat.

Kelsey soon picked up that the two young ladies were romantically involved with the men. One said that she and Dr. Singer had gone to Jamaica recently. The other girl pulled out a joint and offered it to Kelsey. She declined their offer. One of the girls asked Kelsey, "So what do you do?" "I am going to art school." The joint-producing lady stared dreamily and said, "I should go back to school. I always wanted to be a beautician." This led the girls to giggling, at some kind of private joke between the two, Kelsey determined.

At one point, one of the now-high girlfriends turned to Kelsey. "Do you want something stronger?" She reached into her handbag and pulled out various prescription bottles. "I have oxys, Zanax, whatever you want." "Thanks, but no," declined Kelsey.

Kelsey could not wait to return to shore. Four hours later, after a light lunch and conversation dominated by Dr. Singer's description of the even larger yacht he intended to buy, the "Seaduction" returned to the marina. As Kelsey exited, Dr. Singer and

Doctor C had their arms around their lady friends. Dr. Singer told Kelsey they would be in touch.

On the ride home, a frustrated Kelsey asked Taylor, "What was that all about?" An evasive Taylor responded, "They have to be careful. I'm sure they will reach out to you later." Kelsey could not resist asking him about Doctor C. "How come he treats you badly?" But surprisingly, Taylor defended him. "He's really an okay guy. He's been very good to me." Kelsey retorted, "I hope so."

As they drove to the funeral home, Kelsey hoped to get some evidence and tried to engage Taylor in some discussion about his work. But Taylor would not respond. "I can't talk about it right now, Kel." So the couple rode in silence the rest of the way to the funeral home. As she was getting out of the car, Taylor said something unusual: "Be careful, Kel." A disappointed Kelsey left the vehicle focused on the lack of evidence of the opiate business. She later realized she should have paid more attention to Taylor's words.

Chapter 21: Kelsey's "Relapse"

IT WAS A FAR DIFFERENT TAYLOR who picked up Kelsey three days after their boat trip. He had told her that his partners had agreed to let her work with them as a recruiter. She again had asked Taylor to pick her up a block away from the funeral home. She did not want to activate Sonny's suspicions. The key chain would be her only companion once more.

Taylor had a coffee waiting for her. "Double cream, no sugar, right?" Kelsey smiled. When they dated, Taylor used to always pick her up with her coffee just right. In fact, he surprised Kelsey by suggesting they go to a favorite spot in the mountains near the funeral home, a beautiful vista that overlooked Springdale. They had often necked there as a couple.

While they were driving to the mountains, a voluble Taylor explained the pill business to Kelsey. She could not determine if he was excited or nervous, as in rapid-fire manner he told her everything. Taylor confirmed that indeed, Dr. Singer and Doctor C were partners in the pill business. "It's a beautiful thing, Kel. Dr. Singer can write as many prescriptions as we have patients, and Doctor C has people to collect and distribute pills anywhere in the country."

"Your job as a recruiter is to secure people to obtain and pick up the prescriptions. That used to be my job, until I got a promotion. All you have to do is scour the town to get patients. It's so easy, Kel. You can get people at homeless shelters, playgrounds, colleges, and even businesses. If they want to make some money, we pay them $300 to simply go to one of Dr. Singer's offices and get the prescriptions filled. Dr. Singer normally prescribes a dose of 100 pills of 50 mg. oxycodone. That's worth $5,000 on the street. We're doing about 2,000 pills a week, Kel, and you get $500 for every person you sign up. I made $3,000 in one day!"

"That's all you have to do, Kel. You bring the patient to one of Dr. Singer's offices, and he does the rest. You don't even have to take the patient to the pharmacy to fill the prescription. Our runners do that. They go to the pharmacists who are part of our team. The runners then get the pills to the dealers on the streets."

Kelsey was incredulous. "Don't the doctors examine the patients?" she asked. Taylor's look immediately told Kelsey that the whole thing was a scam. "What for? Look, Kelsey, it all works. Some of these patients have insurance, SSDI, and Dr. Singer even gets reimbursed for the office visit. It's so easy."

As Kelsey slowly sipped her coffee, her head was calculating the enormous amount of money and people involved in this opiate business. "No wonder so many people are dying," she thought to herself. "So what's you new job, Taylor?" With a sly grin, Taylor said, "I'm going into the drug rehabilitation business. I'm going to be a different type of recruiter – I'm going to be a body broker."

Kelsey was about to ask just who or what was a body broker when her head started spinning. She tried to say "body broker," but her tongue would not move. She gargled, "Bawdy boker," before the darkness came.

The body broker topic was the last thing Kelsey remembered, high up in the hills of Springdale. The next thing Kelsey remembered was waking up to the genial face of Dr. Knight. "Is this some kind of perverse deja vu?" Kelsey thought to herself. "How are you feeling, young lady?" Dr. Knight asked. A groggy Kelsey looked up. "How did I get here?" "You overdosed in a known drug house – the mix should have killed you, Kelsey," responded the somber doctor. A confused Kelsey tried to piece together how she ended up in a drug house.

It was then Kelsey sensed some movement in the room. She slowly got into focus the concerned faces of her mother and Sonny. They quickly surrounded her on either side of the bed. "How do you feel, honey?" asked Susan. "I'm not sure, Mom." Sonny held her hand, whispering, "I should have never let you go with that guy." They all hesitated on asking the question on their minds – how had she relapsed and ended up in the drug house?

Her wits starting to come back to her, Kelsey said, "Where is my purse?" Sonny disregarded the question. "I've made arrangements for you to go back to the Evergreen residential facility when Dr. Knight releases you, Kelsey." "I agree with Sonny, honey. It's for your own good," her mother said. Kelsey again asked where her purse was. Sonny gently patted her hands. "Have no worries. You just get some rest, and we will be back tomorrow." A reassured Kelsey drifted off to sleep.

The Girl Who Woke Up in the Morgue

In fact, Sonny did not know the whereabouts of Kelsey's handbag. In his concern for Kelsey's welfare, he had missed the significance of what was in the handbag – the testimony from Taylor that outlined the drug scheme.

In the next 48 hours, an increasingly stronger Kelsey pieced together how she was saved. Apparently her notoriety as the girl who woke up in the morgue saved her. That headline and the accompanying photo years ago was somehow noticed in the drug denizen. One of the heroin users in the house noticed the unconscious Kelsey. She had called 911, and Narcon had saved Kelsey's life.

But unresolved for a foggy Kelsey was how she was drugged. She would not, or could not, believe that Taylor was involved. On the third day following her hospitalization, Dr. Knight again said that Kelsey's vital signs were stable. "You know, three strikes and you are out in baseball, Kelsey. I'll make arrangements for you to go to Evergreen in the morning."

Kelsey was ambivalent about going back to Evergreen On one hand, she was focused and confident in her sobriety. On the other hand, these drugs were introduced again into her body, and treatment would be a good reinforcement. The next morning, she was once more a resident of Evergreen.

Chapter 22: Kelsey's Return to Evergreen

KELSEY AGAIN ENTERED the fashionable Evergreen Treatment Center. She was again met by its fashionable director, Dr. Peggy Schmidt. "I know you were here before, Kelsey, but I have to go over our regulations again," said the doctor. In addition to her treatment and activity obligations, Dr. Schmidt reminded Kelsey that Evergreen was a locked facility. No one was allowed to visit after 6 p.m.

Kelsey soon settled into her comfortable unit. She wandered into one of the community rooms and was surprised to see a familiar face. It was Janice, her feisty roommate from the Spring Valley Sober House. "Yup, Kelsey, I'm cycling through again. This is my third time here. My insurance company will not pay for any more treatment, so I guess it's my last visit here," said Janice in her still sarcastic voice.

Janice suddenly stopped chewing her gum, a sign that she was about to say something serious. In fact, this time Janice spit her gum out. "I heard what happened to you, Kelsey. You're lucky to be alive." "I know," Kelsey said quietly. "You know you were set up, right?" A contemplative Kelsey said, "I don't want to believe Taylor set me up." A solemn Janice replied, "He had no choice. He has to do whatever that asshole Doctor C tells him to do. The word on the street is that Doctor C and his partner, Dr. Singer, heard you were investigating them."

A stunned Kelsey replayed the demeanor of the men on the boat. It became clear to her that they intentionally avoided anything about their business. She considered, "Is it possible that they were aware I was trying to record them?"

Janice was not done surprising Kelsey. "Are you aware that Dr. Singer owns this place?" Kelsey was stunned. "How the fuck do you think he affords that boat?" said an ever-frank Janice. "He cycles people like me through this place back to the Sober House in Spring Valley, where he makes sure opioids are readily available. Dr. Singer's accountants

The Girl Who Woke Up in the Morgue

must feel like laundry workers, spin-cycling people over and over again. He has people on the street whose only job is to bring patients here. They are called body brokers." With that, Kelsey remembered the last words Taylor spoke to her before she passed out. "Taylor's new job was to get people here!" she gasped.

Overwhelmed by all the information coming at her, Kelsey soon became fearful. If Singer tried to kill me once, what will prevent him from trying again?" she asked herself. She promptly returned to her room. She speed-dialed Sonny but reached only his voice mail. Desperate, she then dialed Detective LeBlanc's cell, also to no avail. An increasingly nervous Kelsey knew she had to get out of Evergreen tonight. Then she thought of Felix. Hearing her concerns, Felix told her he would be right there.

Fifteen minutes later, Lieutenant Felix Osborn was at the front door of Evergreen. Even he was surprised that his uniform fit so well, if a bit snug. He made sure to include all his impressive badges and citations, including the Navy Presidential Combat action citation, which he rarely displayed.

Felix was forced to ring the bell of the locked facility. He was happy to be greeted with a salute by the security guard. "Good evening, sir," said the guard, "Semper Fi," indicating that he was a former Marine. In his strongest military voice, Felix Osborn said that he had to remove a resident for her protection. The hesitant Marine said he could not open up the facility without approval. "Let me call in…" Before he could continue, Felix said forcefully," I order you to open these doors." The guard hesitated, but then somewhere in his ambivalence he was a Marine again, following orders, and he obeyed. Felix soon had Kelsey in a tight hug. A sobbing Kelsey listened to Felix's comforting words: "It's okay. I'm here."

The shaken Kelsey was soon back at the funeral home. Sonny was distraught. Kelsey reassured him that she was fine. "Where is my purse Sonny, with the recorder? I have Taylor on it telling me about the whole operation, including its head ,Dr. Jerome Singer."

"Dr. Singer," said an incredulous Sonny, "is the leader of this conspiracy?" "Yes," said Kelsey, "And he and his drug-dealing partner tried to have me killed."

Sonny's dismay soon became more evident. "I don't have your purse, Kelsey. I thought I did, but in the turmoil of your hospitalization, it somehow got lost. I even went to the hospital security, but it was never inventoried there."

The Girl Who Woke Up in the Morgue

Felix piped up, "Maybe it's still at the drug house where you were found."

The three individuals were soon before the dilapidated, boarded-up home, in a neighborhood that was once nice. Knocking at the front door, they made quite a sight – a middle-aged funeral director, a lieutenant in full military regalia, and a twenty-two-year-old woman who had nearly died there.

When no one answered, three individuals hesitantly entered the darkened house. The stench of human waste confronted them. As their eyes adjusted to the darkness, they wandered from room to room. Careful to avoid the garbage strewn about, they noticed someone sleeping on a mattress on the floor. Next to him, smoking a crack pipe, was a sad-looking woman. She was in such a stupor, she did not acknowledge the guests.

As the trio continued their search of the house, they observed other addicts. Most were sleeping or just sat staring at the group, showing no emotion. "Oh, shit," said Felix as he stepped in a large pile of human waste.

In the last bedroom was a young woman, seemingly more alert than anyone else in the home. "Welcome to paradise," she said with a bitter laugh. "What is your name?" Kelsey asked. "I'm Sarah." Kelsey moved closer to her, and the young woman whispered, "I know you. You're Kelsey. You're the one who woke up in the funeral home. We all had a big laugh at that – no one is that lucky in this house."

Remembering that day, Kelsey just stared as Sarah continued, "I'm the one who called 911, Kelsey. My cell phone is all I have left that the drugs did not take. They took my kids, my body, and my future." It was then that Kelsey noticed a second object that Sarah clung to-- Kelsey's purse. Sarah held onto to it so tightly that it seemed to be a symbol of a life she once had.

Kelsey held Sarah's hand and thanked her again for saving her life. "Sarah, in that handbag is evidence that might get these drugs off the street." Sarah stroked the leather bag before handing it to Kelsey. "If it saves one life, I'll feel good," she said. A tearful Kelsey then held onto Sarah,.."Come with us. We will get you help." Sarah shook her head, "It's too late for me. Can you give me some money for a bag?"

Sonny and Felix had to pull Kelsey away from Sarah and the wretched house. Kelsey cried on the ride back to the funeral home. "We have got to stop this! We can't leave Sarah." The resolute trio returned to the funeral home, high above a troubled

Springdale. It was time to get outside help for their community.

Chapter 23:
The Criminal Investigation Begins

THE NEXT DAY, A MEETING WAS HELD at the funeral home with the four principals: Detective Skip LeBlanc, Sonny, Felix, and Kelsey. They all listened to Taylor's words emanating from the key chain. "It's a start," said Skip. "I think we can call in the DEA to help us." Felix cursed Taylor, "He only said these things because he thought Kelsey would be dead."

This led to a discussion about how Dr. Singer and Doctor C knew that Kelsey was an informant. Felix deduced that someone around the four of them had received the information. "We all have to be careful." Skip assured Kelsey that they will have a police presence around the funeral home.

The Girl Who Woke Up in the Morgue

Skip then updated the group about the status of his operation. He had set up a security camera at the Greenville Clinic. They had video of up to one hundred people a day getting prescriptions, often given to the same patients over and over. "That tells me they are using false names to get scripts," commented Skip. "One informant told us this Doctor C pays $300 to these individuals per script."

Three days later, the group reassembled at the Springdale Police Department. They were joined by the Drug Enforcement Agency's lead investigator, who would be in charge of the operation. The special agent's name was Randall Gray. Having listened earlier to Taylor's words, and Detective LeBlanc's findings, he slowly shook his head. "Nothing more than greed." He said that this was a typical "pill-mill" operation, where the operation quickly goes beyond the confines of Springdale. "I'm sure these pills are distributed all over the country."

As the group sat at the table, a weary Agent Gray took off his eyeglasses. He was a tall, almost gaunt sixty-year-old with Lincolnesque-like large eyes, with heavy lids that almost hid the iris. He spoke assertively to the group. "We are going to solve this conspiracy the same way it started – through greed and self-interest. We are going to start at the lower levels of the organization and have them turn on each other like ravishing rats. They will then be offered pleas if they provide us with data and information. Eventually we will nail the leaders of the conspiracy, including the doctors and pharmacists, who will serve the long sentences they deserve. I'm hoping to charge them with murder."

The trio of observers were stunned when Agent Gray said that what was happening in Springdale was not unusual. "These pills are a public health menace. Families throughout our country became addicted to pills that came out of their medicine cabinets. I have looked at the literature that the pharmaceutical companies sent to doctors, starting in the late '90s. These companies marketed to doctors and convinced them that their patients no longer had to be in pain. Soon, names like oxycodone, Vicodin and Percocet became household names for safe pain-relieving medications. These companies proclaimed that their new synthetic slow-release pills were completely safe. Even early in this century, when these companies saw that patients were becoming addicted, they kept pushing out pills."

At this point, Special Agent Gray's somber, heavy laden eyes were almost closed. He continued his witness to what he deemed as a grave American tragedy of this new century. "First, the pharmaceutical companies mass produced these pills and marketed them with slick advertisements. 'Americans deserve to be pain free,' they said. Then they solicited the doctors. I put doctors in one of two categories. The majority were careless, some even negligent in not warning and monitoring their patients for misuse. Many doctors simply renewed prescriptions again and again for back injuries that never healed. Some were negligent in handling prescriptions. I recently prosecuted a doctor's medical assistant who was forging the doctor's name on hundreds of prescriptions. Fortunately, these doctors are finally waking up to the danger of these drugs."

"The second type of doctors are the Dr. Jerome Singers of the world. They probably represent only one percent of doctors. The problem is, that one percent can spread hundreds and thousands of pills throughout America. And it is not only for money--I prosecuted a recent case where a pharmacist was trading sex for scripts.

"Up until recently these bad physicians had little risk of prosecution. This has resulted in elaborate conspiracies, which also defrauded Medicare and insurance companies of millions of dollars."

Special Agent Gray then explained the process of the investigation. "Hopefully with the recent evidence we received, within the next three weeks my team of agents will be seizing the records of Dr. Singer's two medical offices. We will similarly obtain all records from the pharmacies we think are involved in Springdale and Greenville."

Agent Gray then turned to Kelsey. "We picked up Taylor last night on an existing motor vehicle warrant. He seemed almost relieved, Kelsey, as the word on the street is that Doctor C was hunting for him. It seems you didn't fulfill your part, Kelsey, and you survived their attempt to kill you. Taylor readily admitted that the coffee he gave you contained crushed fentanyl. He thought that it was only enough to scare you."

Kelsey surprised herself with her reaction. She felt pity rather than anger. This person, her first love, had sold himself for money. The sensitive nature that had attracted her to Taylor had been corrupted. Sonny and Felix comforted her as she absorbed this news.

Agent Gray added, "If it helps, Kelsey, he seems genuinely contrite. He wept in our office and said he wishes he had drunk the coffee himself. At Taylor's request, we also picked up his sister Sophia. He felt she was in danger from Doctor C. Both parties have agreed to fully cooperate with the investigation. Their knowledge of the conspiracy and the players will lead us up the organizational structure. I am confident we will cure Springdale of this scourge."

Detective LeBlanc ended the meeting on a somber note. "I have learned how Dr. Singer heard about our little investigation. Agent Gray informed me that my former chief, Chief Powell, was on Dr. Singer's payroll. He was essentially looking the other way as our community was poisoned. I'm sick, because it does not reflect on the honorable men of my department. Chief Powell will answer for his actions."

As Special Agent Gray had predicted, the city of Springfield was upended in the next week. Dr. Singer and his patients could only watch as federal and state agents arrived at his clinic with search warrants. Within minutes, boxes of records were being carted to police headquarters. Patients who were pain-free in the waiting office quietly walked out.

At the same time, agents in the Greenville office secured the limited records of the patients and their identification data, since investigators believed this was a cash clinic. If this cash clinic resembled others in their investigation, they would see many fraudulent or fictitious names.

The two pharmacy records were also secured. Undercover agents had already filled prescriptions at each address with obviously flawed scripts. The agents were not even asked for any identification from the pharmacists as they received 60 to 100 pills on each visit.

The first person Agent Gray and his team decided to interview was Dr. Singer's longtime office manager, the matronly Delores St. Gelais. Despite appearances, she was known to run the office with an iron fist. Most importantly, she had decades worth of knowledge about the workings of the bustling practice. All of her five-person staff deferred to her, particularly with third-party billings. Off the top of her head, she could address any Medicare or insurance questions.

Mrs. St. Gelais came into Randall Gray's office with an attorney provided by her boss, Dr. Singer. Agent Gray initially appealed to Mrs. St. Gelais's heart. He inquired if anyone in her family had been impacted by opioids. With a nod from her attorney, Mrs. St. Gelais answered negatively. She added that she did not believe doctors were responsible for anyone's addiction.

Agent Gray then turned to his tried-and-true method: self-preservation. "Mrs. St. Gelais, from our preliminary investigation, you are looking at up to ten years incarceration

The Girl Who Woke Up in the Morgue

in the opioid scheme. In addition, your work defrauding the Federal government through Medicare and Medicaid claims can lead to another ten years. Oh, and in addition, it can come with a fine of up to $200,000."

A flustered St. Gelais turned to her attorney and said, "You didn't tell me I was at risk for this." Her attorney stood up and said, "We are done here." "No," said the old woman, "I am not going to take the fall for Dr. Singer." This was music to Agent Gray's ears. At that moment, Mrs. St. Gelais become a cooperative informant.

The next person on Agent Gray's list was Taylor's sister, Sophia. A fearful Sophia readily told the agent about her role in the organization. Her job, given to her by her brother, was that of a "runner". She would go to the designated pharmacy, with or without the patient, and obtain the pills. Some weeks she collected up to 30 prescriptions. Agent Gray did some math in his head. If an average script has 30 pills, Sophia was delivering up to 1,000 pills a week in the Greenville clinic alone. She then shocked Agent Gray and said she knew of three other runners.

Agent Gray then explored what Sophia did with the pills. Twice a week, she delivered the pills to her street dealer, Oscar King. Oscar told her that most of the pills were shipped out of state within twenty-four hours. Sophia said she earned up to $2,000 weekly for her work.

Following his interview with Sophia, Agent Gray offered her police protection. She had been warned by Doctor C to keep her mouth shut if questioned. She feared him, but agreed to testify against him. She named the three pharmacists she was told to see. If these pharmacists were out, Sophia was instructed not to fill the prescriptions. Often they were filled and given directly to Sophia.

Soon, Agent Gray's team brought in Oscar King for questioning. He too was initially defiant. The color seemed to drain from his face as Agent Gray shared his deep knowledge of the conspiracy. "I'm going to give you one chance to work with us, or else I'll get someone else. You are looking at a minimum of ten years for the charges in Springdale. In addition, interstate dealing of opioids had the potential of another five years. You can leave right now, or you can tell us what you know."

Oscar decided to cooperate. He revealed that he reported directly to Doctor C. He had no contact with Dr. Singer. As the top street dealer, Oscar distributed some of the pills to his four dealers in Springdale. Some dealers worked the streets, others went to schools, or even to sober houses like Spring Valley.

The Girl Who Woke Up in the Morgue

The majority of the weekly amount of pills went to Doctor C. Oscar said that they were sent to nearby states within 24 hours. Oscar said that Doctor C preferred selling them in affluent areas throughout the country. Doctor C would brag to Oscar, saying, "Some of these fucking kids with their allowances will pay me seventy-five dollars for a single 50 mg. oxy."

Agent Gray's team spent the next few weeks acquiring information from these three witnesses. They examined forensic records, patient information, and insurance reimbursements. Along with the Springdale district attorney's office, Agent Gray methodically prepared his indictments.

Chapter 25: Operation Spring

ON JUNE 2, 2014, Special Agent Randall Gray stood on the steps of Springdale City Hall. Surrounded by a phalanx of DEA investigators, FBI agents, and local law enforcement, including Detective LeBlanc, Agent Gray announced a series of sixty-eight separate indictments. An array of media members pushed each other to get a better image of the gathering.

He announced that nine individuals, including the two ringleaders, were indicted for operating a drug ring that delivered up to 2,000 opioid pills per week in the Springdale area. Agent Gray announced that eight other individuals had previously pleaded guilty to conspiracy to distribute a controlled, dangerous substance. Kelsey listened to his

The Girl Who Woke Up in the Morgue

words in the company of hundreds of fellow "Springdocians." She realized that her friends Taylor and Sophia were two of those guilty pleas.

The State Grand Jury indictment charged the two ringleaders, Dr. Jerome Singer and Robert Christoyannopoulos, AKA Doctor C, with first-degree conspiracy charges to distribute controlled substances. Agent Gray's heavy lidded eyes more open than normal, he voiced anger at the unprecedented charges. "For the first time in this country, we are charging a physician, in this case Dr. Jerome Singer, with five counts of murder for prescription practices that led to the death of five patients between 2007 and 2020. Each count brings a potential sentence of twenty years to life."

Agent Gray also announced that Mr. Robert Christoyannopoulos, AKA "Doctor C," also faced a first-degree charge of promoting organized street crime. This carried a ten-year sentence. He was also charged with one count of second degree attempted murder against one Kelsey Jordan, in addition to a money laundering conspiracy.

Special Agent Gray continued, "Dr. Jerome Singer has also been charged in a 13-count indictment for healthcare fraud. It is alleged that his medical clinic submitted more than 10 million dollars in false and fraudulent claims to Medicare and Medicaid. He faces a maximum penalty of ten years in general prison for each of the 13 counts. In addition, Dr. Singer was charged with 10 additional counts of insurance fraud for cycling patients through three of his recovery centers: Evergreen, Spring Valley, and the Phillips House. We allege that Dr. Singer and the two physicians in his office routinely sent patients to these centers while also prescribing them opioids. We allege that Dr. Singer earned up to 10 million a year from his multiple enterprises."

"In addition to these individuals, we arrested four doctors and three pharmacists last evening. They will appear in federal court tomorrow. Two of these doctors were members of the Springdale Family and Wellness Center. It is alleged that over a three-year period from 2010 to 2013, this practice distributed over one million oxycodone pills. We allege that these doctors did so with the knowledge that these patients had no legitimate medical reason for the prescriptions."

"We further allege that the Greenville Medical Center was nothing more than a "pill mill" operation. The two physicians indicted today saw patients without appointments who often showed visible signs of addiction. Patients were required to pay hundreds of dollars in cash for each prescription. These doctors often issued the prescriptions directly to "runners," rather than the patients. These runners then distributed the pills on the Springdale streets. We allege that these Greenville doctors continued their prescribing practices even after being made aware that some patients had died of drug overdoses."

"We allege that two physicians in Dr. Singer's office knowingly prescribed unnecessary prescriptions while also ordering unnecessary medical tests. They prescribed medications to individuals who were accompanied by known patient recruiters."

"The three pharmacists involved in this scheme were charged in a separate 16-count indictment. They were charged with conspiracy to illegally distribute and disperse oxycodone and other schedule II substances; maintaining drug-involved premises; and multiple counts of illegal distribution."

"We allege that these pharmacists knowingly filled fraudulent prescriptions. They often prescribed them to known addicts who routinely paid the doctors in cash.

The physicians involved in this scheme "steered" their patients to these pharmacists. These conspiracy charges against the three pharmacists carry a maximum of twenty years in prison and a million-dollar fine."

Agent Gray concluded his statements with the following words: "This is the type of behavior that has resulted in the worst drug crises in American history. The worst villains in this fight are doctors and pharmacists who violated their oaths to 'do no harm.' They were drug dealers in white coats who knew some of their patients would die. And their motive was simple greed."

"The law enforcement personnel you see here today are committed to ending the illegal distribution of opioids in Springdale and our great country. These charges should serve as a warning to medical personnel who act like drug dealers. We will investigate and incarcerate all those who violate their professional oaths."

"Before I conclude my remarks, I would like to thank one individual who helped uncover this conspiracy. Her name is Kelsey Jordan." Kelsey's face reddened as her friends in Springdale turned and clapped. "This young lady showed tremendous courage in pursuing criminal acts which were destroying lives in Springdale. We would not be standing here today handing down these indictments without her help."

The Girl Who Woke Up in the Morgue

A surprised Kelsey did not know what to do. Felix, who was holding her hand, simply raised her hand in acknowledgment. As she lifted her head, Kelsey observed many of the sad faces that she had seen in the funeral home. Moist eyes like that of Jim Fisher, who had lost his son, and many others – sisters, friends, co-workers – who had lost loved ones because of simple greed.

Kelsey wondered how these hundreds, if not thousands of bereaved people felt at this moment. Their community had been intentionally poisoned by a product that had a good purpose. She thought of the callousness of its leaders: Dr. Singer and Doctor C, and the scourge's other victims, Taylor and Sophia.

As all these thoughts permeated her sensitive head, Kelsey became aware that the applause had not stopped. In fact, it grew larger. Soon the people of Springdale, her new home, surrounded her. Mr. Fisher and his family smiled through their tears.

Their son's short life had meaning. Like Kelsey, they would use his death to warn others about the opioid dangers.

One of those clapping was a frail elderly man whose coat collar was turned up so high that his face was barely visible. Sonny recognized his old friend Dr. Stanley Singer, the father of the one Agent Gray held responsible for the conspiracy. As Sonny embraced the elder doctor, he repeated over and over, "I'm so sorry, Sonny." Sonny hugged his friend and reassured Stanley that his son's acts had no reflection on him. When Sonny buried Stanley Singer three months later, the death certificate listed the cause of death as a heart attack. But Sonny knew it should have said, "cause of death: a broken heart."

Chapter 26:
To the Head of the Snake

As Agent Gray had predicted, the Springdale opiate case resembled a domino game. More and more lower-level participants "flipped" in order to get a reduced sentence. Agent Gray doggedly worked his way up to the head of the snake-like conspiracy. His real targets were the two leaders whose sad talents meshed so well – Dr. Jerome Singer and Robert Christoyannopous, AKA Doctor C. Agent Gray knew that many interstate opioid investigations involved these two individuals. The agent's mission was to find out how these pills were distributed throughout the country so efficiently.

Agent Gray and his team allowed some of the street level "soldiers" to plead guilty to one count of illegal distribution of controlled substances. Sophia and some of the street "soldiers" received two-year sentences in return for information. Taylor received a longer sentence of five years for his role managing the street recruiters. He'd escaped attempted murder charges for Kelsey's overdose, primarily at Kelsey's urging. Office manager Delores St. Gelais was given the shortest sentence: one year, which was suspended. Her meticulous records of the insurance fraud were instrumental to Agent Gray's case. Drug dealer Oscar King was not as fortunate. His interstate work led to a four-year sentence.

The three pharmacists and four doctors who were major players in the conspiracy did not receive much sympathy. One pharmacist blamed his actions on his own opioid addiction. Despite his plea for mercy, he and the other pharmacists involved received prison sentences of ten years. The four doctors who worked for Dr. Singer were sentenced to twelve years in jail, as well as fined one million dollars each. All seven of these individuals lost their pharmaceutical and medical licenses respectively.

Robert "Doctor C" Christoyannopolous fled Springdale ahead of the indictments. Two weeks later, he was arrested and extradited from his parents' New Jersey home. It was said

The Girl Who Woke Up in the Morgue

that upon his arrest, his mother, Magda, tearfully told the FBI agents that they had the wrong boy. His father Christo disagreed. He told the same agents that his son turned his back on this great country, which had welcomed his family and given them hope for the future. He asked the agents to tell the residents of Springdale that his family apologized for the pain they had caused.

When Agent Gray finally got a chance to talk to Doctor C, the agent was pleasantly surprised. Unlike Dr. Singer, Doctor C in criminal parlance sang like a canary. He offered a complete portrait of the conspiracy in exchange for a reduced sentence. He agreed to name the distributors of the conspiracy that extended from coast to coast. Doctor C also agreed to testify against his former partner, Dr. Singer. Aware that Doctor C's testimony would help in investigations throughout the country, Agent Gray accepted a plea agreement. Doctor C got a reduced eight-year sentence, with ten years of probation to follow.

Agent Gray watched as the now-convicted criminal Robert Christoyannopolous signed his plea agreement. Even then, the charismatic former athlete tried to work his charms on the F.B.I. agent. While shedding crocodile tears, he blamed Dr. Singer for bringing him into the conspiracy. "I was just a small-time dealer around here. I'm sorry I met that guy."

Agent Gray was having none of his excuses. "I wish you had to face each family that lost a son or daughter because of you, Robert. But that probably wouldn't mean anything to you. Human suffering means nothing to a person like you, consumed with money and riches. I wish I could sentence you to life in prison. The only reason I am agreeing to this deal is that it will save more lives." A chastised Robert simply dropped his head.

On the other hand, a bold and defiant Dr. Singer fought all the charges against him. He acted like he was smarter than those seeking to prosecute him. Up to the trial, he maintained that the charges against him were just a "witch hunt." He pointed to the thousands of families he had helped over the years; people who had benefited from his treatments. Yes, he had prescribed pain medication, but in his mind the abuse was the responsibility of the person taking the opioids.

On the eve of the trial, Federal prosecutors were extremely confident of their case against Dr. Singer. The pyramid of people, from star witness Doctor C to lowly office manager Delores St. Gelais, were prepped and prepared for a lengthy trial. However, this didn't happen. Apparently, Dr.

The Girl Who Woke Up in the Morgue

Singer's team of expensive lawyers got the doctor to see the hopelessness of his case with all the evidence against him. Facing up to life in prison for multiple counts of conspiracy to possess and distribute controlled substances, five counts of murder, and multiple counts of health care fraud, Dr. Singer agreed to the settlement his attorneys negotiated. He was sentenced to twenty-five years in Federal prison. In addition, he agreed to reimburse the government up to eight million dollars for Medicare fraud. Civil litigation by the private medical insurance companies that he'd defrauded ensured Dr. Singer would have little money left when he got out of prison as an old man.

During his sentencing, Dr. Singer stoically looked away as several Springdale family members confronted the disgraced doctor. In a firm voice, Marcia Carson said, "I am Sam Carson's mother. He was only eighteen when you killed him, our beautiful son." She forced the doctor's attention, if only briefly when she raised her voice, "Look at me, Doctor. Our son came to you for an appendectomy, and you got him hooked on these pills. We called you several times to tell you of our concerns, but what did you do? You simply prescribed a different medication. You didn't even respond to us when we told you how violent our son was getting. In three months, we watched how our loving and good son was being destroyed by the pills that you supplied. And now we know that you were destroying families all over the country. I hope to God you sit in your cell thinking about all the pain you caused."

Marcia Carson's last comment got Dr. Singer's attention. He briefly removed his glasses and wiped a tear from his eye.

Fred Carson then spoke. "Your father took care of me as a child. He is a wonderful man. We decided that you would be our family's physician to continue this legacy. Little did we know that you are a selfish, uncaring murderer. You murdered our son with pills instead of a gun. May you rot in prison."

Bereaved dad Bob Fischer spoke to Dr. Singer about his son. "You never met my son Robert Junior, Jerome, but you killed him." Commenting that called him a doctor would insult good doctors like the senior Dr. Singer, Bob continued, "My son got pills from his fellow band members; pills you put on the streets. In fact, these kids were so addicted that they took pills the night of my son's funeral. Yeah, that's right, Jerome. My son lay in a casket while his friends consumed pills in the funeral home. They so needed those pills that they lost all human ability to be respectful at their dead friend's funeral. And you said these pills are not addictive. You are a disgraceful human being."

Before sentencing, Justice Andrew Stearns asked Dr. Singer if he had anything to say. Dr. Singer's only reply was, "I did not kill anyone."

Justice Stearns disagreed. "The public had no knowledge that these new opioid pills were dangerous and addictive. We know that now. America was deceived by the drug manufacturers who made billions while lying to the public. But you, Dr. Singer, cannot hid behind the anonymity of Big Pharma. You saw the damage being done to these families – families that you took an oath to protect. Instead, you chose money in your pocket over any concern for others. You will have years to ponder why this lack of character led to blood on your hands."

Chapter 27: Chief Powell's Revelation

LT. SKIP LEBLANC, still groggy from a 6 a.m. wake up call, did not recognize the number. Letting it go to voicemail, he picked the phone up immediately when he heard that the location was Amesbury Federal Prison. To his surprise, he heard the voice of his former boss, Chief Frank Powell, the disgraced former chief of police in Springdale. This year, 2015, Chief Powell was one year into his ten-year sentence for multiple counts of corruption. The former chief was guilty of looking the other way as Dr. Singer and Doctor C corrupted the community. In his pact with them, he also agreed that for a $5,000 monthly fee, he would destroy opiate evidence which may have revealed their conspiracy years earlier.

The Girl Who Woke Up in the Morgue

"How are you doing, Frank?" Skip asked, speaking coolly to his former boss.

"Not well. I have plenty of time to dwell on how I violated my oath, Skip. My wife and kids want nothing to do with me, and I don't blame them. I am deeply remorseful. I'm now part of a religious men's group here that has really helped me. That's why I'm calling you, Skip. I need to clear my conscience about something else. Can you come up here to see me? I only trust you with this information."

Skip was used to the forceful voice of his former boss, who in the past acted like the citizens of Springdale worked for him. But today, Frank's voice had an almost childish plea in it. Almost sympathetically, Skip responded, "Sure, Chief."

The next day, Skip drove the two hundred miles to the out-of-state Amesbury Federal Prison. Skip knew that Frank's placement at the prison was not accidental. Law enforcement prisoners, especially former chiefs, were not popular among the inmates. The ride gave Skip time to renew the guilt he had tried to forget since Chief Powell's admissions. He murmured to himself, "Why didn't I pick up on the chief's lack of attention to Springdale's growing drug problem?" His thoughts then turned to anger at the violation of his profession. His anger swelled when he thought about how Chief Powell had relayed Kelsey's undercover role with the department to his criminal partners. Skip was determined to confront Frank about that.

Skip LeBlanc did not have to worry about that. After processing through the modern federal prison where inmates slept in pods rather than cells, Skip sat alone with Frank Powell. The man before Skip was no longer a burly ex-Marine with the military gray butch cut and perfectly tailored chief's uniform that could fit the cover of GQ. That man was gone. Instead, before Skip sat a frail man with deep purple circles around his eyes. Frank was perhaps 55 years old, but to Skip the man looked about 70, and his weight loss accentuated his wrinkles.

Frank spoke first. "Thanks for coming, Skip. I know you probably feel disgust for me. No more than I feel for myself. I pray for forgiveness every day, and..." Frank could not complete the sentence. He lowered his head as he covered his face and sobbed into his grimy hands, hands that in the past had been perfectly manicured. His hands remained over his face for an uncomfortable period of time – until the sobs turned into deep sighs.

Frank continued, "I'm part of a men's religious group here, Skip. Pastor O'Neil leads

The Girl Who Woke Up in the Morgue

us. He's a really wonderful guy. The group had forced me to examine why I became a criminal. I think it all came down to pride, Skip. Pride and money. I believed I was above the law, and that allowed me to justify almost all of my actions. I told myself that the town did not appreciate my work, and I was underpaid. Once I did one small favor for those guys, it was easy to rationalize other acts, until I had become a criminal. How could I have been so stupid?"

"I don't understand, Frank. How could you jeopardize our investigation of those guys, Frank? It was the ultimate violation of your oath, and you almost killed that poor girl, Kelsey."

Frank forced his hands over his face again. "I know, I know. I'm so sorry. I pray to God every day, thanking Him for saving that young girl."

Trying unsuccessfully to hide his disgust, Skip advanced. "Why am I here, Frank?"

"Well, my pastor has helped me to see that I have to be completely honest to seek forgiveness. I am involved in other crimes, involving the Fultons."

"You mean George and Harry Fulton?"

"Yes. Over the years, I looked the other way when they committed some building violations. You know the low-income housing the Fultons rehabbed over in Southport a few years back? "

"Sure, that was a big job awarded to them by the town."

"Well, I helped them get that project. I told them what the competitor's bids were. It was not a fair process."

Skip shook his head, "How much did they pay you for that?"

"They paid me $50,000. It's all with the attorneys now. But that's not all. While rehabbing those buildings, the Fultons encountered all types of asbestos. George came to me. He said it would cost them a fortune to dispose of it legally. So I let them bury it in a nearby marsh."

Skip pondered the location – so those kids in Southport were playing near that shit?

"Yes," said Frank, looking away.

Skip had to get away from his former colleague. "Is this why I'm here, Frank? So you can feel better about yourself?

"No," said Frank, "I have one more confession." Frank took a deep breath and began, "A few years back, George Jr. came to my office. He asked me to take a ride with him. He seemed nervous and upset. He told me that a judgment had just been rendered against the Fulton brothers for ten million dollars in an out-of-state lawsuit. It involved a class action

The Girl Who Woke Up in the Morgue

suit regarding a subdivision that the Fultons had built. Due to drainage issues and a faulty levee design, the homes had flooding problems after each storm. George said this was 'bullshit', but he never mentioned that he had promised the homeowners his company would build a levee, a project he'd severely under budgeted."

Frank continued, "Anyway, George said that the only way out was to get his hands on his mother's multi-million dollar life insurance policy. He said his mother was on her way out anyway. He asked me to get him some strong sedatives, because he didn't want 'those assholes' Dr. Singer and Doctor C to know what was going on."

Skip realized at once why George had approached the chief. The police evidence room was loaded with all kinds of opiates – some pills up to 80 mg. One pill could easily kill an elderly woman like Mrs. Fulton. He stared at the chief and said, "So you helped kill her as clearly as George did. Are you willing to testify to what you did?"

"Yes," said Frank. "I need to clear my conscience. I'm prepared to die here – it's what I deserve. I only hope that God will forgive me one day."

Standing up and happy to leave, Skip addressed Frank, "Okay then, I'll call the district attorney's office in the morning. You will sign an affidavit giving us all the details."

"Yes," replied a sitting Frank.

"Good. I'll be in touch soon," said Skip, leaving without a further word.

Chapter 28: The Fultons Guilty of Matricide?

As Lt. LeBlanc drove back to Springdale, he had plenty of time to think about the Fultons. Their building legacy in Ridgewood was pristine. In addition, they were prominent citizens, who were often the first in line to give to charities. Although Skip remembered that they always wanted the public to know about their philanthropic activities. George Fulton Junior, the more outgoing of the brothers, would have his picture in the Springdale Times each week for one endeavor or another. His brother Harry seemed not to prefer the limelight as much.

Skip knew that prosecuting the Fultons for their mother Grace's death would not be easy. They would secure high-priced attorneys, who would use the media to create doubt. However, Skip felt that with Frank Powell's direct testimony, the district attorney prosecutors would prevail. He planned to call his friend Sonny Fiorentino to exhume Grace's body, and hopefully the drugs would be found.

Thoughts of Sonny triggered thoughts of Kelsey, who still lived in the funeral home. "Poor girl," he thought. "She has been through so much. Now I have to tell her that her uncles may have killed her grandmother."

Three days later, state prosecutors with prepared affidavits returned to the prison to secure the confession of Frank Powell. Dispatched hazmat workers identified asbestos fibers in the area of the Fultons' Southport project, the area identified by the former chief. This finding lent credence to Powell's charges.

One negative was that Skip had learned since Grace Fulton was cremated, there was no drug to investigate. Sonny Fiorentino recalled how surprised he was when the Fultons requested an immediate cremation of their mother. Given their prominence in the community, Sonny knew that hundreds of Springdale mourners would have wanted to pay their respects to Grace Fulton.

The Girl Who Woke Up in the Morgue

Skip was surprised that Kelsey took the news of her grandmother's homicide death so well. " I knew something was off the day I met my uncles in the funeral home," she said. "They almost acted like they were guilty of something. At the time, I presumed they felt guilty because they were always too busy for my grandmother. Uncle Harry, in particular, could not even look me in the eye." Kelsey added something that got Skip's attention. "If you need information about how my uncles ran the company, contact Ruth McGrath." Kelsey recalled her old boss at the Fultons' company when she moved to Springdale. "She ran that company like a drill sergeant. My uncles depended on her for everything. Ask her about the Christmas bonus."

"Christmas bonus?" asked Skip.

"Yeah, every year she complained that the Fultons gave her the same meager bonus, year after year."

Four days after his interview with Frank Powell, Lt. LeBlanc and two prosecutors drove to Amesbury Prison. Confessions in hand, the team was stopped by tragic news. Frank Powell had been found dead in his cell, an apparent suicide. He had tied bed sheets from a doorframe, and soap on the floor ensured a tight noose. The prison superintendent told

Skip that the prison would investigate the case further.

"I can't believe it," said Skip to the team. "He seemed so sincere that he wanted forgiveness from God. And God does not condone suicide."

"Maybe it wasn't a suicide," voiced one of the prosecutors, airing something that everyone was already considering. Had the Fultons silenced Frank Powell?

Skip's mind immediately turned to the ramifications of the absence of the primary witness. "We still have charges on the illegal dumping of hazardous waste, correct?"

"Sure," said the prosecutor. "It's a federal offense, and the civil litigation could go on for years."

"Okay then," said Skip, "let's prepare the basic indictments against the Fultons. I'm going to talk to the Fultons' secretary.

Ruth McGrath walked into the Ridgewood Police Station at the request of Detective Skip LeBlanc. The sixty-year-old woman had been retired from the Fultons for two years. Never married, the trim woman with the ramrod posture marched in a crisp manner to the desk of the detective.

"I can't say I've ever been part of an investigation," said Ruth on hearing why she was there. She responded to Skip's question in a perfunctory manner – indifferent, as if she was fulfilling a duty. No, she had not seen illegal actions by the Fultons. Yes, she kept the books for the Fultons. No, she did not see suspicious deposits. Yes, she had seen the Fultons with Chief Powell, but she saw them with lots of politicians also.

Frustrated, Detective LeBlanc recalled Kelsey's words about Ruth's Christmas bonus, or lack of it. "So, the Fultons paid you well for your services?" he asked. For the first time, Skip saw a type of "reveal" that poker players look for. "It was adequate," said Mrs. McGrath crisply, adding, "I worked for them for thirty years."

"How about your Christmas bonus, Mrs. McGrath? Most companies show their appreciation to their employees for a year of good work."

"Do you believe the Fultons gave me a meager thousand dollars each Christmas. It never increased for thirty years, while they made millions. After everything I did for them, that's what they thought of me."

Detective LeBlanc never had to say another word. For the next hour, Mrs. McGrath regaled him about her intimate relationship with the Fultons. "Half of the time, they didn't even know I was in the room when they talked. I was like the wallpaper."

Mrs. McGrath revealed that there were many other incidents involving buried or transported asbestos – often in open trucks. She told the detective that the Fultons did not want to pay to have it removed legally. She smirked as she repeated George's words: "I'm not going to make the EPA rich." Mrs. McGrath disclosed that Chief Powell came to the office once a week, usually on Fridays, and she even witnessed the Fultons give him an envelope filled with cash. Most importantly, she verified that the Fulton Company was hemorrhaging money prior to her retirement. "They even had their kids on the payroll, with no-show jobs."

Skip could not believe his good fortune. "Would you agree to testify to what you told me, Mrs. McGrath?"

"Of course," she replied. "I always complete my civic duty."

Armed with this testimony, Detective LeBlanc decided to call in the Fultons for questioning. He was not surprised that the brothers arrived with their respective high-priced attorneys. Detective LeBlanc insisted on interviewing the brothers separately.

George Fulton Junior's attorney, Harry Sherman was a top longtime criminal attorney in Springdale. An aggressive, almost pompous man, he was barely settled in his chair when he jumped up and said to his client, "We are out of here!" His reaction came from Detective LeBlanc's comment that he was investigating Grace Fulton's death. Turning to the detective, Mr. Sherman said, "I believe any lying witness you may have has died."

"Not so," said Detective LeBlanc calmly. "Plus, we have evidence that your client was illegally dumping hazardous waste for years."

"Come on, George," Attorney Sherman said as he buckled his law briefcase. "See you in court."

Harry Fulton sat in a separate office with his attorney, a younger member of Attorney Sherman's office, Attorney Diedre Cummings. Perhaps because she was less experienced, or less pompous, she did not stand up when Detective LeBlanc told them why they were there. In fact, when Harry Fulton heard the reason was about his mom's death, he bowed his head.

Picking up on the body language, Detective LeBlanc went to work. "Harry, I am going to give you one chance to come clean here, and if you do, you will get a reduced charge. We know the Fulton Company has been illegally dumping waste for years – that alone will get you twenty years in prison. We know you guys were having financial problems, and that subdivision judgment was going to put the Fulton Company out of business. Your mother's insurance money was your only way out.

Head bowed, Harry Fulton started to talk. "No," said Attorney Cummings, "Don't say another word. We are out of here, Detective." But Harry Fulton did not move.

"Sit down, Diedre. I've suffered with this every day since my mom died. I knew it was wrong. It didn't matter that her health was failing. We still killed her."

And with that, Harry supported the testimony of the late Frank Powell. "We put her to bed after giving her the pill, and within an hour she stopped breathing. It was very peaceful. I told myself that she had a good death. I don't care what happens to me now. I had to tell someone."

As Harry's dispirited attorney threw a pen on the desk, Skip LeBlanc felt relieved that he had solved Grace Fulton's murder.

Epilogue

In 2015, Sonny Fiorentino no longer got up as often at 3:00 am to pick up opiate victims, but he continued to have people of all ages succumb to death from pills. Sonny could not understand this, since new restrictions nationwide had limited availability of these pills. In fact, the restrictions were so rigorous that Sonny, who had recently had knee surgery, was told he could have nothing stronger than Tylenol.

Sonny now had people to take care of him. Although he remained unmarried, he had two tenants, similar to his old friend Kelsey, who kept him company. One of the young ladies was the gum-chewing Janice, the addict who had befriended Kelsey at the Sober House. Now, two years into her recovery, she had needed a place to live when first released from a treatment center. Sonny welcomed

Janice into his home with the same terms he had given Kelsey. She never left.

Janice was a forceful presence in the busy funeral home. In addition to vacuuming rugs and removing flowers, she had a rare talent for helping the bereaved. Her levity and wit often left mourners smiling and saying words such as, "My dad would have loved you."

Janice brought such joy to Sonny that he overlooked the one thing that's anathema to funeral directors: gum on the rugs! For funeral directors, gum on their pristine carpets is a menace. Bubble gum, Janice's favorite, was the worst.

The second young woman living in Sonny's funeral home was Sarah, the haunted girl in the drug house who had helped save Kelsey's life; the young girl whose only physical possessions were a cell phone and the infamous purse. Both objects were instrumental in saving countless lives in Springdale, especially Kelsey's.

Sarah Young, sober one year, was now a healthy, robust college student. She would soon become a drug counselor. Sonny gladly paid that tuition. Something about his profession always drew Sonny toward helping the living.

And finally, Springdale had a new resident: Kelsey's mom, Susan. She was now

The Girl Who Woke Up in the Morgue

known as Susan Fulton. "I want to bring respect back in this town for my family name." She had moved to Springdale to be near her daughter, but frankly, she could live wherever she liked. Susan Fulton was a very rich woman. The life insurance for her mother had to be paid to the only heir not in prison. She now drove a Jaguar and carried a different color Gucci purse every day.

Susan was not completely refined, however. She no longer uttered profanities of any sort, but there were some occasions when the old Susan emerged. Whenever she saw her former sister-in-laws on the Springdale streets, she gave them a middle finger before scooting away in her gold Jaguar.

As for Kelsey, she was now known as Kelsey Osborn. Yes, she was the wife of Felix Osborn, who had rescued her from the treatment center. A true May-December romance, the couple, now married for three years, still acted like newlyweds.

If you are ever in Springdale, look for Sonny's funeral home. You can't miss it. Look for the highest ridge in town. The stained glass windows color the sky like a rainbow. If you should venture in, you are likely to see a dark-haired young woman in one of the chapels. She will be behind an easel with her paint brushes. At her feet will likely be a rambunctious two-year-old with curly hair the color of her own. This child is Kelsey's son, Felix Orazio Osborn.

Kelsey has a new job. Every family that Sonny buries receives a portrait of their loved one. The young lady who almost died in the morgue below her invariably receives a hug for her gift. They always praise the artist for "capturing" the essence of their loved ones.

Lt. Skip LeBlanc often visits Sonny's funeral home, and the two reminisce about the scourge that almost destroyed their community. Both realize that the opiate problem has not entirely gone away. Skip often recalls one of his last conversations with DEA Agent Randall Gray. Yes, Agent Gray died of a silent heart attack shortly after leaving Springdale in 2012 to clean up another pill-mill operation.

Looking particularly weary one day after Dr. Singer's conviction, Skip asked, "Why so gloomy, Randall?"

"This snake is not going away; it's simply changing its shape." Agent Gray explained that while law enforcement was clamping down on the bad doctors and their prescriptions, the problem was going underground. "A black market is emerging with counterfeit pills made both in and out of

The Girl Who Woke Up in the Morgue

America. They look like ordinary pills, but can be laced with any strength of opiates. Worse, more and more of these pills have deadly doses of fentanyl." Skip never forgot Randall's last words. "At least when doctors were prescribing these pills, we knew what these kids were getting. This problem is not going away. Fentanyl is relatively easy to make, profitable, and very transportable. We are now finding fentanyl labs in this country."

Sonny now understood why he was still burying victims of drugs. In fact, from the death certificates, he realized that many of the recent deaths did not have traditional opiates like oxycodone or hydrocodone. He told Skip, "Most of the deceased I work on died of heroin that had been laced with fentanyl." Skip agreed, "They are adding drugs like fentanyl to anything – cocaine, heroin, even marijuana. These kids don't know what they are taking anymore." Sonny concurred, "I'm burying good kids who might have made one mistake – these drugs do not offer second chances. I wish everyone could see the grief that accompanies these deaths." As Sonny said this, he pulled out a copy of the only poem he had ever written:

Stephen Rocco

<u>A Funeral Director's Wish</u>
I wish you could see
What your late brethren have taught me
No decisions are left
Shame and regret no more

I wish you could listen
To the guilt and anguish
That is your legacy
An eternal weight on those left behind

I wish you could hear
The echoes of your death
"So much to offer" "So much to love"

I wish you were me
Learning lessons from fateful decisions
Of choosing to embrace a high,
Left
A world denied your talents

Postscript from the Author, Stephen Rocco

MY NOVEL EXAMINES America's opiate problem in the mythical towns of Ridgewood and Springdale from a far different societal perspective than today. Back at the turn of the century, only those affected by opiates were witness to this growing epidemic. The lies of big Pharma and the greed of a small number of doctors and pharmacists impaired our knowledge. But as the fictional, but prescient DEA Agent Randall Gray predicted, the problems have only gotten worse. It is only fitting, then, that I quote from a DEA Public Safety Alert dated September 27, 2021:

"The DEA warns the American public of the alarming increase in lethality and availability of fake prescription pills containing fentanyl and methamphetamine.

International and domestic criminal drug networks are mass-producing fake pills and marketing them as legitimate prescription pills."

The alert states, "More than 9.5 million counterfeit pills were seized so far this year, which is more than the last two years combined. DEA laboratory testing further reveals that today, two out of every five pills are laced with fentanyl."

The article further quotes this sad statistic: "According to the Centers for Disease Control and Prevention, more than 93,000 Americans died of drug overdoses in 2020. Fentanyl is the primary driver of this alarming increase in overdose deaths."

America must unite and be vigilant in educating the public about the dangers of these drugs. As Sonny Fiorentino, and all funeral directors, witness each day with mourners: "These drugs do not offer a second chance."

ABOUT THE AUTHOR

Stephen Rocco is a third-generation funeral director in a funeral home outside of Boston. In addition to working as a funeral director over 40 years, he was a family mediator. He was an instructor at Mt Ida College for many years and Co -Director of its National Center For Death Education. Stephen and his wife, Lidia, have been blessed with four children and three grandchildren (and hopefully many more).

CPSIA information can be obtained
at www.ICGtesting.com
Printed in the USA
BVHW081308210622
640289BV00002B/108